THE STORY OF MY LIFE
by Shayna

As Told to Greta

(With Comments by
Murphy, J.J. & Greta)

Written by
Greta Marsh

THE STORY OF MY LIFE – BY SHAYNA
As Told to Greta *(with Comments by Murphy, J.J. & Greta)*
By Greta Marsh

Published by 1st World Library.
For information, please contact:
    1st World Library
    8015 Shoal Creek Blvd., Suite 100
    Austin, TX 78757
    www.1stworldlibrary.com

DISCLAIMER:

Many of the characters in *Part One* of **The Story of My Life – by Shayna** are fictionalized. Any resemblance they may have to individuals alive or dead is coincidental.

The American Greyhound Racing Association and *The National Greyhound Advisory Council* are fictionalized names.

Although some of the events described are based on facts, some are not and *Part One* is a work of fiction.

ISBN: 1-887472-95-9
LCCN: 2003100443

Graphic design and text formatting by Sharon A. Dunn, Treefrog Graphics.
Printed in the United States of America.

Dedication

To involuntary athletes everywhere and
to all living beings, regardless of species,
who have been and continue to be the
victims of human greed and cruelty.

And

To the late Dorothy Checci-O'Brien,
lobbyist, passionate advocate for animals
of other species, and a woman of valor.

*Proceeds from the sale of this book will be
used to aid and rescue animals in need;
other-specied animals as well as human animals.*

Acknowledgments

We wish to express our deep appreciation to
Rodney Charles of 1st World Library for believing
in Shayna's story; and to Sharon A. Dunn for her skills
in graphic design and text formatting. Among other
things, Sharon designed our book's beautiful
cover. To both of you we say Thank You.

– Shayna, Murphy, J.J. and Greta

Epigraph

God Has Implanted Mind and
Instinct in Every Living Being.

– Hebrew Prayer

What is Hateful to You,
Do Not Do to Any Person.

– Torah

What is Hateful to You,
Do Not Do to Any Living Being.

– Shayna

Table of Contents

Introduction

The story of my life is about dog racing and a good deal more. It is about cruelty, the human capacity for cruelty towards human animals and animals of other species. Dog racing, commonly known as Greyhound racing, is not a sport because no legitimate sport uses enslaved/involuntary participants and murders many of them once they start losing and no longer are competitive and profitable. Dog racing is, in fact, a deadly form of entertainment, as are horse racing, dog fighting, cock fighting, hunting and circuses that use enslaved other-specied animals.

Incidentally, I remember Greta talking about a form of entertainment that was popular in Ancient Rome and which took place in public arenas. There enslaved humans known as gladiators were forced to engage in deadly combat against each other to the delight of cheering crowds. Often the losing gladiator was killed outright, and sometimes he lived depending upon the mood of the spectators.

Unlike some spectator sports whose fans identify with and form emotional attachments to the athletes, dog racing fans care little or nothing about the Greyhounds. This detachment can be attributed to the racers' short racing careers; some race for just one season or part of a season at a specific track, and then are shipped elsewhere.

But let's return to my story. Please know that I am real, as are other characters. On the other hand, some characters are not real. They are fictional. And although some of the events discussed in Part One are based on real happenings, some are not, and Part One is a work of fiction. In conclusion, I hope with all my heart that this book touches the hearts and minds of its readers.

– Shayna
Lanesboro, MA (1998)

PART ONE

THE STORY OF MY LIFE
– by Shayna

(Chapters 1 – 18)

 Abandoned

This is the story of my life. It begins with a kind stranger, a compassionate animal control officer, a Greyhound rescue/adoption group, and a wonderful new family. The story of my new life begins with an ending; it begins at the end of my racing career and at the end of a terrifying ordeal I thought surely would signal the end of my life. The story of the end of my old life and the beginning of my new life starts harshly on a bitter cold day in Massachusetts in November 1992, when I was almost four years old. In fact, I was just six weeks shy of my fourth birthday, which is considered old for a racer. It's a day I'll never, ever forget. It's the day Sam, my trainer, the man I thought cared about me, abandoned me.

On this particular day he told me to get into his truck. It was a pickup truck, not the kind he used when he transported us from one track to another and from one state to another. This one had plenty of fresh air and, since I thought he liked me a lot because I'd won lots of races and money for him, I jumped in without hesitation or fear. He said we were going for a ride and I was excited because that was far more pleasant than lying in my cramped crate for twenty or more hours a day. I remember wishing he'd remove my racing muzzle because the bridge of my nose was sore and hurting. But he didn't, and I decided not to ask. They were made of some hard material and we were supposed to wear them only while racing, but my friends and I wore them almost constantly. They were awfully uncomfortable.

It was a brisk, sunny day and the drive was quite pleasant. I remember how the rays of the sun touched my body, warming it and making me feel content and peaceful, feelings racers rarely feel. Sam continued driving until we came to a cemetery. Then he stopped the truck, got out, and told me to get out too. I did, thinking the two of us would go for a walk. But then without saying a word, Sam jumped back into the truck and sped away. He left me there. Alone. On a cold, winter day. Still wearing my racing muzzle. Did he forget to remove it? I thought he did, but later on I learned that abandoning muzzled, no-longer-profitable racers was not an uncommon practice. Now all I could think about was that the man I thought was my friend had abandoned me. Without even saying good-bye.

I tried to run after him, but a line of sleek black cars with their head-lights on stopped me. By the time they passed, Sam's truck had disappeared. Being a sight-hound who depends more on her sight than sense of smell, I knew I'd never be able to find him. I was stunned. For several minutes I was numb and unable to think. As the shock began to subside, I felt frightened. Terribly frightened. But I was no stranger to fear. As a racer, I'd felt it many times; once when I saw a trainer beating and kicking a racer after she lost a race. No one tried to stop him and he could have killed her. Perhaps he eventually did kill her. I don't know. I experienced fear again during a fire at a kennel compound where I was living. I'll tell you more about that later.

Being terribly frightened I began to tremble and my teeth started to hit each other, making funny, clicking sounds. I told myself not to panic because Sam surely would return. He would. Of course he would. We'd been together for a long time, ever since I started racing at commercial tracks when I was eighteen months old. Whereas most racers are retired at age two, sometimes three, I was still racing while I was almost four.

2 The Beginning

I think I should start at the beginning. I was born near New Ashford, MA, in January 1989. I don't know the day. I was one of seven puppies born to my mother and father. They were former racers who were retired to a breeding farm once their racing careers came to an end. They must have raced pretty good, otherwise they wouldn't have been used to produce more racers. Seven puppies are considered an average sized litter. Some litters are smaller, and some Greyhound mothers have as many as twelve puppies in a litter.

My mother was lovely. I remember that clearly. She was brindle and white and her eyes were exquisite, so exquisite they touched the soul of a four-month-old puppy. I'll never forget her. I don't want to forget her. Not ever. Her name was Star. Mom was always tired. She had no energy. She was worn out and with good reason. When she was just six months old she started training, which is hard work and lasts for a year. It's strenuous work with no time off to be a puppy. After completing her training, mom started to race, although I don't know for how long. Perhaps a year, perhaps two. I don't know. Once she stopped being competitive she was retired to a breeding farm. Back in the 1980s, there were few rescue/adoption groups, and each year about 50,000 Greyhounds would be put to death. Some were retired racers and some were pups who didn't show racing potential. So my mother was given a reprieve of sorts, but at quite a cost.

She was forced to make babies. Constantly. I don't know how old she was when I was born, but if she was young she didn't look young. And if she wasn't young she shouldn't have been forced to make babies. But regardless of how old she was, my mother was beautiful. And I know she loved us because she cleaned and kissed us often, and there always was an expression of love in her exquisite eyes. I was just a puppy, but my mother's lack of energy worried me. So did her sadness, and as I grew older I learned she had good reason to be sad.

You see, many of her babies were destined to die premature and unnatural deaths. She had heard that half the puppies who are bred and born to race never reach a commercial track; that most are killed before they are eighteen months old.

The owner of the breeding farm was a man. His name was Ted. I don't know much about him. Just his name and that he had the power of life and death over all the Greyhounds who lived on his farm. For that reason alone I didn't like him. I disliked him even more because he forced my mother to have one litter of puppies after another and was responsible for her constant exhaustion; her sadness too.

"Breeding was an important part of the human slave industry, too," explained Greta. "Slaves were always needed to work in the fields, so females were forced to breed with males who had certain physical characteristics. The object was to sell them to other slave holders for plantation work or as servants."

"But that's what they do to us," said J.J., Shayna's dear friend. "And I don't just mean Greyhounds. Puppy mills come to mind, as do factory farms, where so-called 'food' animals are bred; likewise horse farms and fur farms ."

"Don't forget those who are bred for sale to circuses, canned hunts and research labs," commented Murphy, Shayna's long-time companion and close friend. "But getting back to African-American slaves, it's all so similar. Once they were looked upon as nothing more than marketable goods. Other-specied animals still are."

Now Shayna spoke. You're right, all of you. Slavery is an abomination regardless of species and it affected me when I was a very young puppy.

When I was just three months old I became aware that two of my siblings were missing. There were only five of us when there should have been seven. I asked my mother where they were and she made no reply. Instead she cleaned me and kissed me and spoke to me gently. "Play my sweet child. Play while you can." I don't believe I ever saw a smile of joy on my mother's face. Whenever she smiled it was to hide her sadness, and when I was older I learned the truth behind her sadness. Newborn puppies whose bone conformation indicated they didn't have racing potential were routinely put to death. I believe they were murdered by being thrown against a wall or having their tiny, delicate heads smashed with a hammer.

As I grew older I understood my mother's sadness even more. She, who knew everything there was to know about this cruel industry, who knew what had been done to some of her new born babies and what was in store for her as yet unborn babies, was unable to save them. She couldn't protect them. The awful truth is my mother and father were slaves, and slaves have no control over their own lives or the lives of their children. Slaves are powerless. Like slaves everywhere, my mom and dad and their children were at the mercy of humans who lacked a conscience, humans who had no conscience whatsoever. Slavery is unconscionable and when ever and where ever it's practiced, children are routinely taken away from their mothers and fathers and families are torn apart.

I understood this at a young age and as I grew older I learned it wasn't just my family that was at the mercy of humans like Ted. All Greyhounds who are born to race are. Then as the years passed and I grew not just older but wiser too, I learned that human slavery in the United States was abolished in 1865, but the enslavement of animals of other species is alive and well. Everywhere. Then one day I learned that in some parts of the world humans continue to be enslaved. I don't understand the human species, but I do understand the agony of mothers and fathers everywhere, regardless of species, when they're forcibly separated from their children. How painful it is.

"Slavery is an abomination regardless of species," commented Murphy.

"Unfortunately, it's been with us for thousands of years," said Greta. "The Roman gladiators are just one example. But slavery wasn't racist. Unthinkable yes, but it wasn't strictly racist. The enslaved gladiators were of the same race as their enslavers; and African, Asian and Arab slaveholders often were of the same race as the persons they enslaved. I believe that only in the United States was slavery a racist thing. And you're right Shayna, in some parts of the world slavery is still a part of the human scene."

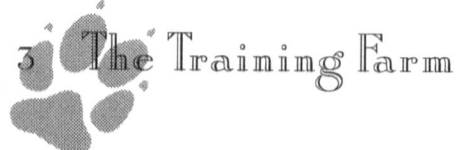 3 The Training Farm

When I was six months of age I left the breeding farm with some of my siblings and about fifty other puppies. Our destination was a training farm in Florida. I'd never see my mother again. Not ever. I try not to think about her because it makes me feel sad and depressed. Young as I was, I loved her and worried about her; my lovely mother whose exquisite eyes touched her young child's soul.

We made the journey by truck. The driver sat in front and we were confined in small, individual compartments in the back. There was no heat or air conditioning in the back, so in cold weather we almost froze, and when it was hot it was unbearable. It was July and very hot when we left Massachusetts. There were no windows in the back of the truck, just slats, so we couldn't even see outside and we had difficulty breathing.

It was a long journey to Florida with little food or water and no rest stops. The compartments were so small we could barely move. By the second day I felt sick, and when we arrived at the training farm many puppies were sick and three were dead. One of my brothers was among the dead. At first I was numb, but once the shock subsided I cried for days. I cried for my brother and the two other dead puppies, and I cried for the puppies that had been put to death shortly after birth, including one of my brothers and sisters. I cried too for the puppies back on the breeding farm because I felt something terrible might happen to them.

Why was there so much killing? I didn't understand it and it frightened me. With the passage of time, I learned that something awful did happen to the puppies back on the breeding farm. They were killed. Some were killed because Ted felt they lacked the physical attributes necessary to make good racers, others because he felt they were too slow, and still others because they were too playful, which Ted felt indicated they wouldn't be serious about racing.

The same weeding out/killing process would continue here at the training farm during the various stages of training. After I had been in training for just six months and was just a year old, I understood that dog racing was serious business, so serious it didn't permit puppies to be puppies.

"Why did you have to train in Florida?" asked Murphy. "Why couldn't you train in Massachusetts, where you were born?"

I used to ask myself that question Murphy, and one day I learned the answer. Some breeders and trainers want their puppies to be trained using small, live animals. They believe the animals' screams and the smell of their blood make the puppies run faster. In Massachusetts, training with live lures isn't legal, so many breeders and trainers send us to other states for training.

"Does that mean training with live animals is legal in Florida?" asked J.J.

No, J.J., it's not legal in Florida. Nevertheless, live lure training takes place in Florida, where there are many training farms, as well as in other states. The industry claims that only a very small percent of trainers use live lures, but I don't believe it. I was just a puppy but I knew it was wrong to harm another living being and the screams of the rabbits who were being torn apart pierced my soul. So I pretended to chase them, but I didn't. In fact, I believe their screams prevented me from running as fast as I might have. Other puppies felt the same. We ran without ever touching a rabbit, yet fast enough to fool our trainers and complete each stage of training.

Others weren't as fortunate. Those who wouldn't chase the rabbits and were too slow disappeared. Those who did chase the rabbits but were too slow also disappeared. This weeding out/killing/disappearing process starts at birth and continues throughout our racing lives. And when our racing careers come to an end, some of us get adopted, but I believe more of us are put to death than are adopted.

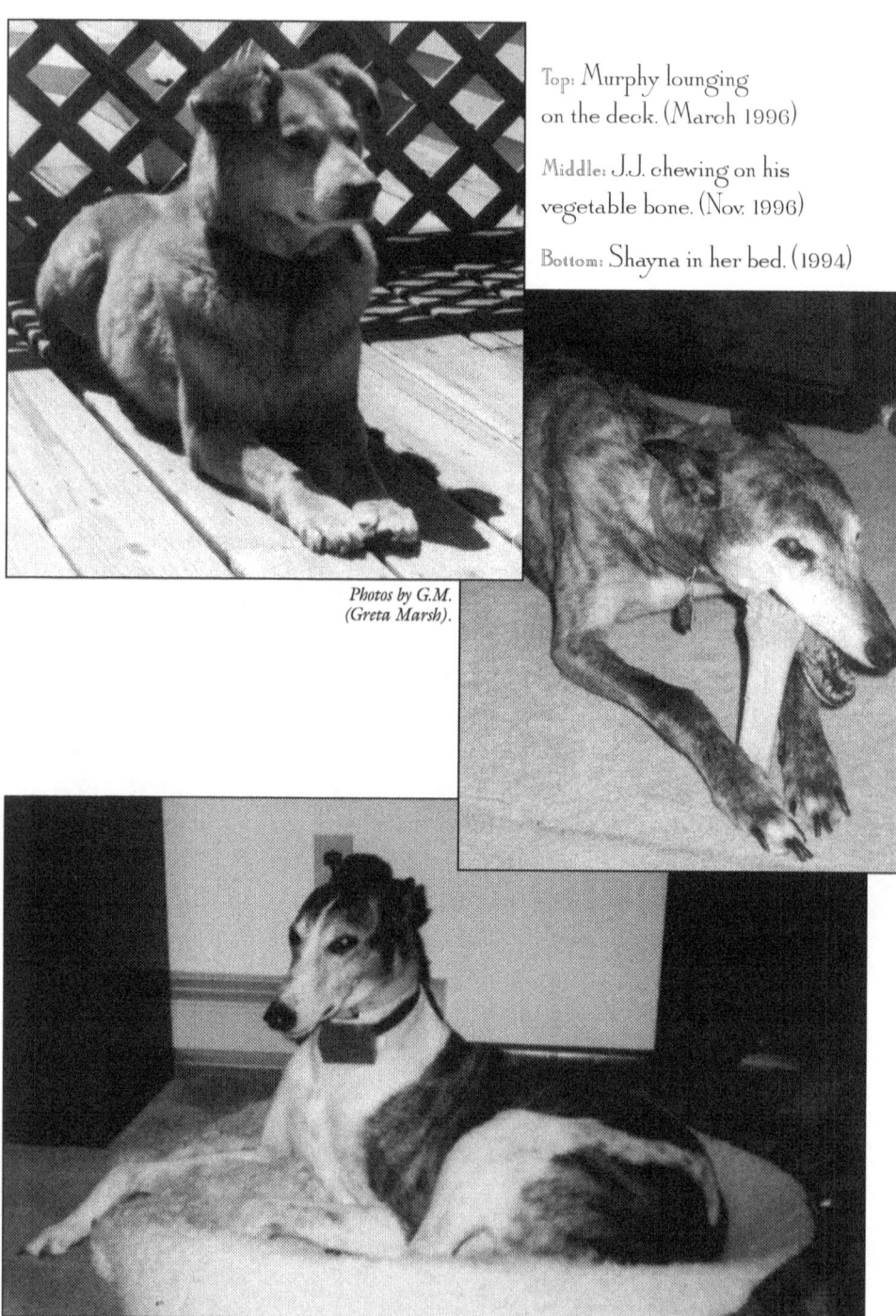

Top: Murphy lounging on the deck. (March 1996)

Middle: J.J. chewing on his vegetable bone. (Nov. 1996)

Bottom: Shayna in her bed. (1994)

Photos by G.M. (Greta Marsh).

4. Sam

During my last stage of training I observed a man watching me closely. His name was Sam, and after I completed my training he leased me from Ted, the breeder in Massachusetts. This meant they'd both share in my winnings, but since Sam was paying for my care and upkeep, he'd keep 65% of my earnings and pay Ted 35%. He wanted to lease my sister too, but another kennel operator bought her. Sam didn't have enough money to buy either one of us. What a strange species humans are. They lease and buy cars, which is ok. There's nothing wrong with that. But to lease and buy living beings? That's not ok. There's something wrong about that. Very wrong. Humans don't see it that way. They don't see the difference between cars and living beings. This is why animals of other species desperately need a Bill of Rights of their very own. But more about that later.

Sam was a trainer and kennel operator who spent half the year in Florida and the other half in New England. After completing my training, I went to live in one of his kennels in Florida, which housed about forty racers. It was located in a compound at the track and Sam's was one of twenty kennels in that compound. Whenever the compound is located at the track, as most are, the kennel owners pay rent to the track owner. When the compound is located away from the track and is privately owned, the kennel operators pay rent to the owner of the compound. For instance, the compound in Lynn, MA, which reportedly houses more than 1,000 racers from one of the Massachusetts tracks, is privately owned and located away from the track.

Before qualifying to race at a commercial track, I first had to compete in some preliminary races. Schooling races first, then maiden or introductory races, both of which I competed in successfully and was classified as a B racer. That's pretty good considering that A is the top classification. I was ready to start my racing career and a part of me was excited, perhaps a bit proud. But I was frightened too and filled with anxiety. I knew I'd never see my mother again, or my brothers and sisters. And I didn't know what lay in store for me. I believe I can say I was more frightened than excited.

 5 My Racing Career Begins

It's not easy to make friends at a kennel because dogs are constantly coming and going and disappearing. It seems you can't have one without the other. I was learning more and more about this industry. For instance, I learned that racing careers can be as short as a few weeks or months, or as long as three-and-a-half years. That means a few race until they're four or five, but they're the exceptions. Most are retired when they're two or three, some even younger. I learned that retirement is mandatory at age five, but not many live to be five. I suppose I was one of the exceptions. I raced for more than two years, until I was almost four.

I learned that retirement can mean many things: death, adoption, sale to tracks in other countries, or sale to research laboratories. This isn't the case with humans. When they retire, their lives aren't at risk. And while they're still in the work force, if their employers should become dissatisfied with them, the worst they can do is fire them. But that's not the case with us. We have no control over our own lives because we're considered somebody's property.

Some trainers abuse their Greyhounds when they lose a race. Sam wasn't like that. He didn't kick or beat us, but he didn't show us any affection either. There were so many of us he didn't have the time to be affectionate. Besides, if he gave himself permission to love any of us, it would be too difficult to dispose of us when we stopped being competitive and profitable. Sam was an unhappy man. He was divorced, which wasn't surprising because dog racing was his entire life. He worked long hours and he worked hard, and he was constantly traveling from one track to another in Florida, or to a variety of tracks in New England. His wasn't an enviable life. But neither was ours. And he chose to live this kind of life. We didn't.

"Then why didn't he get out of the dog racing business?" Murphy asked.

I asked him that question too, Murphy, and I'll tell you why a little later. Because we were constantly traveling, we constantly had to adjust to life in a variety of kennels in different compounds at different tracks. Many of them weren't pleasant. We were confined to small, uncomfortable crates for anywhere from eighteen to twenty hours a day. Sometimes even twenty-two hours. At some compounds the crates were made of wood, or wood and wire. Some were in poor condition. And because they were stacked one on top of another, sometimes the urine from the upper crates would drip down into the lower ones. It was awful, but it wasn't the racers' fault. And when the wooden crates got soaked with urine, nothing could get rid of the awful stench. Nothing! It wasn't easy breathing air that was filled with ammonia, and it surely couldn't have been good for our lungs.

"I've heard that at some kennel compounds the outdoor runs are filled with feces and urine, and racers are forced to stand in the waste."

I've heard that too, J.J., but fortunately I never experienced it. That's probably because I was an A racer for almost my entire racing career.

It was hot in Florida, unbearably hot. It was too hot to race. But we raced anyway, even when the temperature soared to over 100 degrees. I didn't like it. None of us liked it. But we had no say in the matter. We didn't like exercising in such extreme heat either. But exercise is essential if we're to maintain good muscle tone. Without it racers are more vulnerable to injuries. While I was designated in Grades A and B, I was exercised regularly and had excellent muscle tone. But C and D racers aren't as fortunate. They're considered expendable and not worth the extra time or effort. Since the only exercise they get is when they're racing, many of them sustain serious injuries on the track and some are put to death.

"How often did you race?" Murphy asked.

For the first two years I raced about every third day. But some racers race every other day. That's not good because the body needs time to repair itself; one day isn't enough. Racing thirty-five to forty miles an hour for forty seconds or slightly more or less is more strenuous than you can imagine. Competitive racers, those in Grades A and B, are supposed to race only every three or four days, they're exercised regularly, and they receive better care than non-competitive racers. But there are far more non-competitive than competitive racers.

And as they drop to lower grades, their care deteriorates accordingly. Sometimes they're fed raw meat from diseased animals because it's cheap. It smells and tastes awful, but when you're hungry you eat whatever they give you. This meat is dangerous because it's infested with life-threatening bacteria. For instance, *E-coli*, which sometimes causes fatal kidney failure in racers. I remember the pained look on Sam's face the first time he fed me some of this bad-smelling bad-tasting stuff. It was after I lost two consecutive C races. I remember the pained look on his face when I became ill and I remember him saying to me, "Don't let me down, Lady. Please don't let me down. I need you." I didn't understand why he said that when, by his own admission, I was becoming a liability.

Sometimes unprofitable racers aren't fed. They're left to starve to death. Others receive no veterinary care. Adoption groups and shelters report that some arrive in poor condition and health. They suffer from malnutrition, and or broken bones, and or open and festering wounds, fleas and ticks, and intestinal parasites. Since profits are the industry's top priority, it's considered foolish and wasteful to spend money on dogs who don't earn their own keep.

It certainly was hot in Florida. Unbearably hot. Nights were a little better because the sun no longer beat down upon us. But the humidity was intolerable. Heat stroke wasn't uncommon and some of my racing companions collapsed and had to be carried off the track. Some died almost immediately. Others suffered seizures and had to be hosed down. Sometimes this helped and they recovered; sometimes it didn't help and they died. And sometimes those who did recover never raced again. They were never seen again. They just disappeared.

There are more dog tracks in Florida than anywhere else in the world. There are seventeen. And when we finished racing at one of them, we'd move on to another, always in Sam's hot, uncomfortable truck. His horrid, windowless truck. It was so hot that some of us became quite ill, and sometimes after arriving at our destination one or more of my racing companions would be dead or near death. Death was always nearby, especially in Florida. Although weeding out and killing racers takes place wherever dog racing is active, it's probably worse in Florida because there are so many tracks there; likewise, many breeding and training farms. Track injuries are common because of the dangerous turns at some tracks and because some racers aren't exercised regularly. And because of the excessive breeding, which means there are always plenty of youngsters waiting to start their racing careers, it's cheaper to discard injured racers instead of treating their injuries.

So each week truckloads of injured and other no-longer-profitable racers would be delivered to local shelters, where they were put to death and then either cremated or trucked to mass graves where they were buried. The death toll was high. Each year it included hundreds of racers from just a single Florida track. At one track in particular the death toll was seven or eight hundred a year. Multiply these numbers by seventeen tracks and that's many thousands of young Greyhounds murdered in just one year in just one state.

The death toll is even higher when you include those who are sold to racetracks in other countries, to research laboratories, and those who are put to death by shooting, bludgeoning and other cheap and painful methods. The decaying bodies of murdered Greyhounds have been found in a variety of isolated areas, and sometimes one of their ears has been cut off so their *owners* of record can't be identified. But more about that later.

With death constantly nearby, I'd think about my family; the mother I loved so dearly, and my father. Were they alive or dead? Did Ted sell my mother to a research laboratory when she no longer could produce puppies? Was that her fate? And what had become of her other children, my brothers and sisters who started their racing careers at the same time as I? Were they still alive? Or had they too been put to death? Had any of them been sold to research laboratories? Knowing the fate that awaited her children, how could my mother not be sad? And how could I not be sad, too?

I didn't like racing in Florida, but I didn't like leaving either because it meant another journey in Sam's truck – a long, long journey north to New England. We usually spent July through December in New England, racing in Rhode Island, New Hampshire, Connecticut and Massachusetts. Whereas Florida days and nights were unbearably hot, New England winters were bitterly cold. Temperature extremes are difficult for Greyhounds to tolerate because we don't have enough body fat to protect us from the elements. Whereas the bodies of most other breeds consist of about 35% fat, in Greyhounds it's only about half that amount.

Nevertheless, we raced in the bitter cold, in ice and sleet, and sometimes it was so bad I could barely see the track turns. Some of those turns are quite dangerous even in fair weather. They cause torn and stretched muscles, fractures too. I remember slipping and falling on the ice, but each time I was able to get up and continue racing. Other weren't so lucky. They suffered broken bones and couldn't get up. They had to be carried off the track and I never saw them again… They too joined the ranks of the disappeared ones.

When I asked Sam what became of them, he said it was expensive to repair broken bones and he and other kennel operators didn't have that kind of money. That's all he would say. He didn't answer my question. He didn't have to. I understood.

"I understand too," said Murphy. "It's cheaper to discard injured and no-longer-profitable racers instead of treating their injuries because there are always plenty of younger racers waiting to start their racing careers. And Sam and other trainers didn't even have to buy them. They could lease them."

That's right, Murphy. But I felt somewhat bad for Sam. He was having a hard time. His former wife was suing him for back alimony and he hadn't seen his children in over a year. He didn't have enough money to pay all of his bills, which is probably why he started feeding his C and D racers that contaminated raw meat. Murphy, you asked why Sam didn't leave the dog racing business. I once asked him why he didn't find a job that offered a steady and decent income, a job that included benefits for him and his family. I wanted to say a job that did no harm, but thought better of it. He said he didn't have the skills to do anything else. I said he could be trained to do something else. He didn't reply. Our conversation was over.

6 Don't Let Me Down, Lady

I liked racing better than training because artificial lures are used when racing at commercial tracks; chasing live animals isn't permitted. I was relieved, so relieved that I raced faster than ever and was a pretty constant winner for a long time. After qualifying as a B racer at the start of my racing career, I quickly moved up to grade A, where I remained for almost two years until I was two months past my third birthday. During this time, I won Grade A Sprints in thirty-two seconds, sometimes less, and Distance races in thirty-nine to forty seconds.

I was a constant winner for almost two years, with just a few defeats, but nothing serious enough to drop me to Grade B. My best year was 1991, when I won several Greyhound of The Month Titles at some Florida tracks, and captured the Win title at a Massachusetts dog track with twenty-seven victories, twenty-two of them consecutive. As I said, I rarely lost a race until two months after my third birthday. It was then that I lost three consecutive races, each by a fraction of a second, and dropped to Grade B.

"Don't let me down, Lady." He always called me Lady. I told him I was doing my best; that I'd always done my best.

I remained a B racer for a few months. Then, when I was almost three-and-a-half and was racing in Massachusetts, I lost two consecutive races by a fraction of a second. If I lost the next race I'd drop to Grade C. Sam made it quite clear that wasn't a good idea.

"Right now your best isn't good enough," he said. Sam spoke matter-of-factly, without a trace of emotion, like he would speak to a stranger with whom he had no emotional ties. "There's no room in this business for losers. You know that, Lady."

How could he say that? How could he forget the two years that I was a constant winner? Everyone slows down eventually, I told him. Not just Greyhounds. Humans slow down, too. No one can remain a winner forever. No one. The big difference, I told Sam, was that when humans slow down their lives aren't at risk. But when Greyhounds lose by even a fraction of a second they become candidates for a bullet, a metal pipe or worse...

"I'm not interested in excuses or long conversations, Lady. Just don't let me down." That's all he said, "Don't let me down."

I was lucky. My next race was a short one, a Sprint, and I came in third. I was still a B racer. But a month later I dropped to Grade C after losing three consecutive B races. And the following month, in November 1992, I lost three consecutive C races, each by just a fraction of a second. That's when things started falling apart. That's when Sam abandoned me.

I know he cared about me. In his own strange way he cared about me. And I know he didn't have much money and couldn't afford to keep me any longer now that I had become a liability, a financial burden. But why abandon me? He could have placed me with an adoption group. I'll never understand why he didn't. This is something I'll never, ever understand. He didn't have the heart to kill me, but did he think he was doing the right thing by abandoning me in a cemetery in winter? While I was wearing my racing muzzle? Did my more-than-two-year winning streak count for nothing?

Humans are a strange species. They say they're better than we are. They say they're reasonable and rational beings who know the difference between right and wrong. But it's one thing to know the difference between right and wrong and another to act accordingly. Some trainers do act accordingly and are leaving the industry. They're the ones with a conscience, the ones who know dog racing can't be changed, can't become ethical and benign. A few years ago a former trainer at a New England dog track admitted to a reporter that most racers don't live past their third birthdays. That's quite an admission.

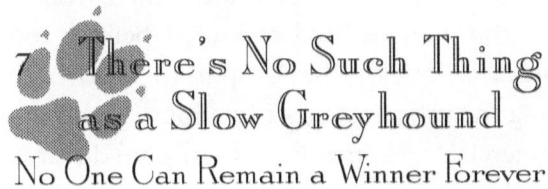7 There's No Such Thing as a Slow Greyhound
No One Can Remain a Winner Forever

People believe that C and D racers are slow, but they're not. They still run like the wind. It's just that they've lost a few consecutive B or C races by a second or less. Let me explain. Our races are short. Quite short. Even the longest is under a minute. Sprints are the shortest at five-sixteenths of a mile. Distance races are a little longer; they're three-eighths of a mile. Marathons are seven-sixteenths of a mile and Super Marathons are the longest at nine-sixteenths of a mile. The average time for running a Sprint is about 32 seconds and the record is a little less; it's about 30.08 seconds. The average for the Distance is about 40 seconds, while the record is about 36.92 seconds. The average for the Marathon is 44 seconds, with a record of about 42.04 seconds. The Super Marathon's average is about 58 seconds; with a record of 57.00 seconds.

This means that the difference between winners and losers and life and death can be just a fraction of a second. To win a race you have to come in first, second or third place. Losing three consecutive races by coming in after third place drops a racer to a lower grade. But that doesn't mean he or she doesn't run fast. It just means that new and younger racers are faster. For example, an A racer has raced the Sprint in 31.57 seconds, and a D racer has raced it in 31.85 seconds. That's a difference of just 0.28 of a second! Yet everyone thinks D racers are slow. They're not. In fact, there's no such thing as a slow greyhound. But even if there were slow ones, our lives would continue to have value.

Yes, our lives continue to have value even after we stop winning. The industry disagrees and kills many of us. It apparently believes winners should live and losers should die. But since no one can remain a winner forever, racing Greyhounds are doomed from the moment they're born. Of the puppies bred to race, I believe about half never reach a commercial track. They're put to death either shortly after birth or during the various stages of training. As for those who do make it to a commercial track, many eventually are discarded; some sooner, some later. It doesn't matter how many races we've won, or how much money we've won, or how many Titles we've captured. We're doomed from the moment we're born because no one can remain a winner forever.

8 The Beginning of My New Life

Back in the cemetery it was bitter cold, already dark, and strong winds were blowing. I was still hoping Sam would return because if he didn't, I'd surely freeze to death. Starve too. I was certain I'd die because I never learned any survival skills. Furthermore, I was wearing my racing muzzle, which would prevent me from eating and drinking even if I was lucky enough to find something to eat or drink. The muzzle hurt; it rubbed against the bridge of my nose, irritating it and causing a good deal of pain. But as my face grew numb from the cold, I didn't feel the pain. I did feel terror, and I wanted to believe Sam wouldn't abandon me so heartlessly. But when darkness fell and he didn't return, I knew he never would. In spite of the years we spent together and all the money I had earned for him, he abandoned me. And without even saying good-bye.

Was I foolish to believe he cared about me? Did he care only about the money I'd won? And when I stopped winning did he think my life no longer had any value? Perhaps that's why he never allowed himself to become attached to any of us. You mustn't allow yourself to grow fond of someone whom you sooner or later will discard. That's the nature of dog racing. What Sam had just done to me wasn't an isolated incident. I'd learn that racers had been abandoned before, sometimes while they too were wearing their racing muzzles. I'd learn that they were still being abandoned and would continue to be abandoned wherever dog racing is active, and that when they "slow down" by that second, or fraction of a second, they're discarded and replaced by new and younger racers.

"And there always are plenty of them," commented J.J., "because over-breeding and dog racing go hand in hand."

Yes, J.J. And that's why the adoption groups, which save thousands of lives each year, can't save all of us. There are just too many of us.

Days passed, or it might have been weeks. I don't know. My face was so numb the muzzle no longer hurt me and I was certain I'd either freeze to death or die from starvation and dehydration. I started to cry. Although dogs can't cry tears, we do cry. I cried so hard that my body started to shake. I was frightened, but I was angry too. How dare Sam treat me or anyone else so cruelly and heartlessly! It started to snow. It snowed hard. I was glad because I was terribly thirsty. I discovered that by rubbing my face in the snow it would pass into my racing muzzle and I could swallow it. It tasted delicious! But I was hungry too, and cold, very cold. And I felt very tired and very, very weak.

One morning I saw a cat who appeared to be dead. I was sniffing the cat through my muzzle when I heard someone scream, "Call the police! There's a mad dog eating a dead cat!"

She screamed it a few times and I wanted to tell her that I wasn't mad and I wasn't trying to eat a dead cat. I wanted to tell her that even if I wanted to, I couldn't eat the cat because I was wearing my racing muzzle. Feeling absolutely helpless, I started crying again. I was still crying when a woman pulled up in a van.

She started talking to me and asked me to get into her van. She seemed nice, but I didn't trust her. How could I? So even though I was tired and weak, I started to run away from her. She got out of her van and tried to follow me on foot, but I kept running and she couldn't keep up with me. Not bad for a weak and discarded racer. When I no longer heard her footsteps, I peeked from behind a tall tombstone and saw her sitting on a small headstone. She was out of breath, as I was.

She was crying too, and later she told me she was crying from exhaustion and despair. Exhaustion from chasing me – despair because she might not be able to save me from a police officer's bullet.

Knowing I couldn't keep on running much longer, I wanted to believe that her tears were a sign that she cared. So I decided to take a chance and trust her. I walked over to her and cautiously placed my head in her lap. She smiled, stroked me gently and spoke to me softly. I followed her to her van and she helped me climb in. Then she removed my racing muzzle. What a relief! I kissed her and licked her in gratitude and she hugged me. I was almost four years old and no one had ever hugged me before. What a wonderful feeling it was! It made me feel warm and loved and so very special.

This wonderful lady was an animal control officer. Her name was Anna, and she's responsible for the beginning of my new life. She told me that a kind stranger had phoned and told her that the police had been summoned to the cemetery to shoot a mad dog. The caller begged her to hurry and rescue the emaciated Greyhound before the police arrived. Anna didn't know the identity of this kind man, but I'll be grateful to him forever. And to her. These two kind people saved my life. If not for them, I wouldn't be here today telling the story of my life.

Anna brought me to a warm and comfortable place and nursed me back to health. She told me she had seen and rescued lots of starving dogs, but I was the worst. Just skin covering bones, she said. That's all. Just skin covering bones.

I recovered rather quickly and a few weeks later Anna brought me to a rescue/adoption group in Hopkinton, MA. It was founded by Louise Coleman in 1983, and is one of the oldest Greyhound rescue/adoption groups in the country. Everyone there was wonderful: the staff, the volunteers, the veterinarian, and Louise herself. Until Anna, I'd never experienced such gentleness and kindness. Surely no one could ask for more.

But the very next day Greta visited Greyhound Friends and, after the veterinarian examined and vaccinated me, I went home with her. But first she pledged in writing that I'd be spayed once I settled down and felt comfortable in my new home. My good fortune overwhelmed me. At my new home I met Murphy, who's part Akita and part Golden Retriever. You ignored me for a few days, Murphy. Remember?

"I'm sorry, Shayna…"

That's ok, Murph, because soon we became friends, then good friends, and after that we became best friends. Your life hadn't been easy either. You, too, had been abandoned. Tell us about it, Murphy.

"One day my humans, I mean the people I thought loved me, moved away and left me behind. They left without any warning and without telling me why. Without finding me a new home and without even saying good-bye. Incredible as it seems, it happens all the time. Our humans, the persons we trust, abandon us. For about a year I lived on the streets. Then one day, someone caught me and brought me to a shelter. I was put in a cage. This confused me because I'd done nothing wrong. It didn't make sense. It still doesn't. But go on, Shayna. I'll explain more about me later."

After a few weeks, you and I started having fun together. Your favorite game is throwing a small rug into the air, catching it, and then throwing it back into the air again. You do this over and over and over again. And Murph, you like to get up early in the morning. Sometimes you try to wake me up by sniffing me and poking me. But I like to sleep late and I tell you so with a growl and a bark. Let me be, I say, because when I get up is up to me. But I love you, Murphy. I really do. And I know you love me too.

"That's right, Shayna. I do. Very much."

For a while it was the two of us and Baron, a handsome former pacer; Baron's buddy Minh, a two-year-old calf who thought he was a horse because he had been raised with horses; Georgie Boy, a three-year-old Thoroughbred just off the track; and of course Greta. Then, about two years ago, in February 1996, a large twelve-year-old brindle Greyhound became part of our family. His name is Jay, but we call him J.J. He's a lucky Greyhound and he'll tell you why.

"I'm lucky because I never raced. My mother and father were racers. They were racing in Vermont when my mother became pregnant. That wasn't supposed to happen because female racers are given steroids on a regular basis to prevent it from happening. I was born in a veterinary hospital in Berkshire County, MA, and when I was about eight weeks old, the veterinary technician who attended my birth adopted my mother and me. For many years I lived the good life, but when I was seven, my mom died. That pretty much devastated me. And when I was almost twelve, circumstances forced my adoptive mother to give me up. I know this was hard on her because she cried a lot."

It must have been difficult for both of you, J.J., not just your adoptive mother. And even though you appear to have adjusted to and accepted us, we don't know what you're feeling and thinking deep inside. But we love you, and in spite of your advanced age J.J., you're still quite handsome. Pretty active, too. And you know, don't you, that Greta calls you our wise, elder statesman?

As for me, Greta said she named me Shayna because in Yiddish it means pretty. But I'm more than pretty, she tells me. I'm friendly in a shy kind of way and very loving. Elegant and funny, too. That's what she says. And she constantly tells me how wonderful I am – by the way, I hear her tell you guys the same thing – and I tell her I'm no different than other retired racers.

She also tells me that if not for me, no bills would have been filed to ban dog racing in Massachusetts. She says I was her inspiration. What a compliment!

"A well-deserved one," commented J.J.

"Yes, a very well-deserved one," agreed Murphy.

Former racer Georgie Boy with Shayna and Greta. (Oct. 1996)

Photo courtesy of G.M.

FORMER PACER
MEETS
FORMER RACER

At Right: Baron,
the pacer, and
Shayna, the racer,
with Greta. (1996)

Below: Baron, a
former pacer.
(May 1996)

Photo courtesy of G.M.

Photo by G.M.

GRETA'S FIRST
RESCUED CALF

Photos courtesy of G.M.

Stair-stepped, from Top:
Minh, the son of a dairy cow,
was born on Nov. 4, 1994. He was
taken away from his mom three
days later These photos were
taken the next day. (Nov. 8, 1994)

Photos courtesy of G.M.; top photo by Elaine Nash.

BARON
& MINH

Left: Baron and seven-month-old Minh. (May 1995)

Bottom: Steve Baer and Baron, with Mary Kelly and Minh in the background. (Aug. 1996)

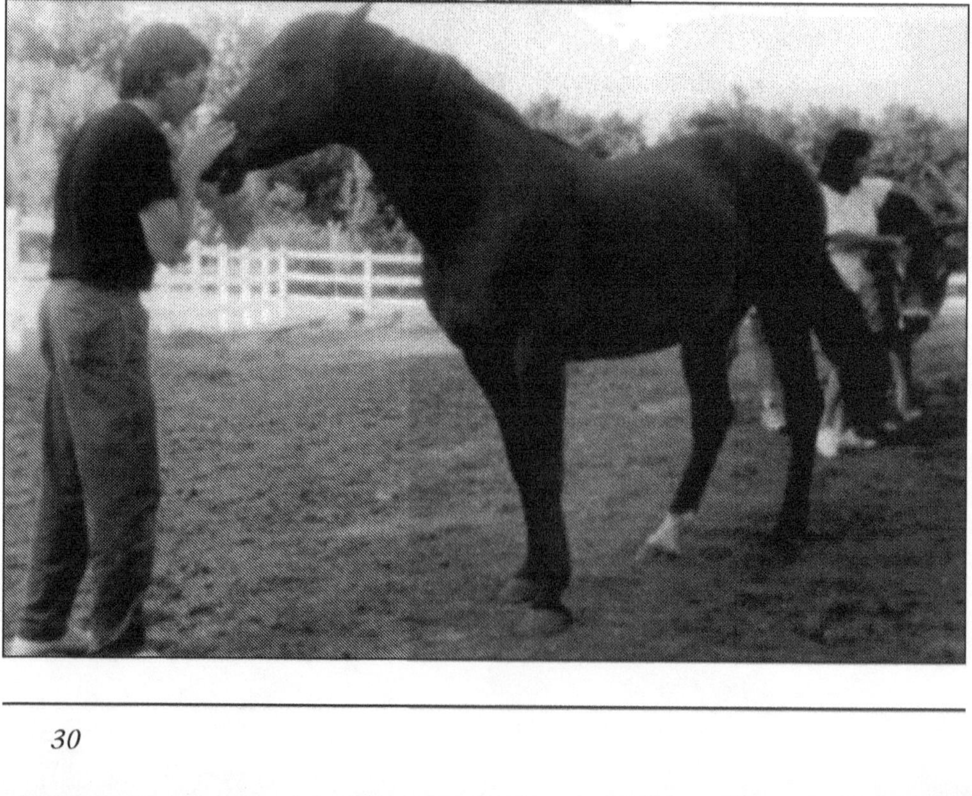

Right: Greta's son David with Baron. (Sept. 1994)

LETTING BARON GO...

Below: The day Baron left for his wonderful new home with his new guardian Sue Kelly (Feb. 25, 1997)

2-25-97

Top Photo by G.M.
Bottom Photo by Sue Kelly.

9 The Disappeared Ones

One day Greta told us that it's not just Greyhounds who disappear. Humans disappear too, she said. She explained that in some South American countries cruel and harsh governments have been known to steal people from their homes, work places, and sometimes while they're walking on the street. They're never heard from again and there's evidence they've been tortured and murdered. They're known as the Disappeared Ones. Greta understands that I almost was a Disappeared One and that some of my racing buddies and many thousands of other racers still are.

Take Danny Boy, for instance. He was a large brindle fellow who looked a lot like J.J. When we first met, Danny Boy was a B racer and his trainer and everyone else respected him. But in just a few months he dropped to Grade C, then D, after losing three consecutive races in Grades B and C by a fraction of a second. Then he disappeared... I never saw him again. I never knew his racing name, but we called him Danny Boy because his mother and father had been Irish racers. Ireland ... another Greyhound hell. Danny Boy wasn't yet three years old when he disappeared, and I hope with all my heart that he was placed with an adoption group.

But I don't know. I'll never know. But I do know this: he should not have died. He deserved better. We all deserve better. The puppies on the breeding and training farms deserve better, as do the Greyhounds who make it to commercial tracks. With proper care and nutrition, we can live to be thirteen or fourteen – even fifteen years old. We don't want to die while we still have so many years ahead of us. But too many of us die prematurely and unnaturally.

How terrifying it must be to see the needle you know is going to snuff out your life, then feel it being inserted into a vein in your leg. And there's nothing you can do to stop it. You're helpless. Powerless.

Soon you begin to feel weak, so very weak. Then everything becomes a blur. The persons who are snuffing out your life become a blur. Finally, it's all over. You're dead.

I can't imagine and I don't want to try to imagine what it must feel like having a gun pointed at your head, waiting for it to explode. Then it does, and a bullet pierces your skull, splattering it into hundreds of pieces. I can't imagine (and I don't want to try) what it must feel like to have your head and face smashed over and over again with a metal pipe until you're dead or they think you're dead and they dump you in some remote desert or wooded area.

But first they cut off one of your ears, the one with the identifying tattoo, so that the person or persons responsible for this heinous crime can't be traced. Sometimes an ear or a few ears are found and the murderers are traced. Are they charged with murder? No! Do they serve jail time? No! Why not? Because according to law, we're property. Just somebody's property. But let me continue.

I can't imagine and I don't want to try to imagine how it feels to experience death by electrocution. To feel an electric current rushing through your body until it kills you. But not immediately. It takes about thirty seconds. And I can't imagine (and I don't want to try) what it must feel like to be a research object in a laboratory, where men and women in white coats strap you down and dissect your body or break your bones or perform surgical procedures on you even though you're perfectly healthy…

"Shayna, please stop."

No Murphy, I won't stop until the killing stops.

"Shayna, I'd like to comment on the needles that snuff out lives. I believe that lethal injections are a Nazi invention; Adolf Hitler wanted a form of execution that would kill large numbers of persons he considered worthless; the physically and mentally impaired, for instance. And so the 'humane' lethal injection was born."

Greta, no form of execution is humane, and no one should have the power of life and death over anyone else. Getting back to slavery, the 19th century abolitionists knew that slavery couldn't be reformed. They knew it couldn't be made humane. They knew it had to be abolished. We know that slavery is slavery regardless of which species is enslaved. Whether its victims are human animals or animals of other species, slavery is unthinkable.

While racing at tracks in New England and Florida, I heard that sometimes racers who stopped winning also stopped eating. They were confined in their crates and deliberately starved. By the time they arrived at a shelter to be put to death or at an adoption group, they looked like living skeletons. South America has its Disappeared Ones, but so does North America. We're North America's Disappeared Ones. I was one of them, although briefly. But most racers aren't as lucky as I have been. As I said earlier, their lifeless bodies have been found in isolated orchards, desert areas and landfills.

"You're right, Shayna," said Greta. "And in a publication devoted to Greyhounds it was reported that forty-three dead Greyhounds were discovered in a remote area in a small city just outside of St. Louis, MO. Three dead cats and a dead rabbit were also found, who probably had been used as live training lures. Some of the Greyhounds were already skeletons, meaning they probably had been there for several months. Others had been left more recently and the ears of the adult dogs had been cut off so that the persons responsible for these murders couldn't be traced. But most of the dead were puppies, some just a few weeks old. Somebody probably decided that these little ones didn't have racing potential. Since the police haven't been able to locate any Greyhound breeders in the area and since there aren't any dog tracks in Missouri, it's believed that breeders and trainers from Arkansas or Iowa dumped the bodies."

Why Arkansas or Iowa?

"Well, both of those states have dog tracks. In addition, you have to pass through that small city in Missouri when traveling to and from Arkansas and Iowa. There's a large rescue/adoption group in St. Louis that would have taken in all of those forty-three Greyhounds, so this was a case of deliberate mass murder. And it wasn't an isolated incident. It happens often, but usually the bodies aren't discovered.

But discovered or not, whenever this happens, it's a clear cut case of cold and calculated murder."

"But Greta, since we're considered property and property can't be murdered, under the law the forty-three Greyhounds weren't really murdered."

"How right you are Murphy, and there was even a time in this country when it was legal to do pretty much the same to black slaves. There was a time when white humans could beat black humans to death, burn them, skin them, and hang them. And it wasn't murder. It was perfectly legal because they were the property of other humans."

You'd think formerly oppressed persons, regardless of their color, ethnic origin or gender, would want to help us. But it just doesn't work that way. And no matter how much I try, I can't stop thinking about the puppies who never made it to a track, many of whom were killed, and Danny Boy and the others who did make it to a track, many of whom also were killed. I think about racers who are forced to race in all kinds of weather, in the extremes of heat and cold and in dangerous ice and snowstorms. Some die from heat stroke and heat exhaustion. Others die from winter injuries and illnesses. Shayna paused, then continued.

I thought about them on the night of November 14, 1997. That was the One Million-Dollar Greyhound Night of Stars, in which eleven dog tracks participated, including one in Massachusetts. Its purpose was to rekindle an interest in what one sports magazine described as a "dying industry." I worried about them because that was the night of the terrible ice storm. Even though the storm was expected to keep large numbers of people away from the track, Greyhounds were forced to race in the freezing rain and sleet. Racing in ice storms is dangerous and scary. I know. How well I know.

I remember one storm in particular. It happened many years ago at one of the New England Tracks. I can't recall which one. I was scheduled to race in a Distance event and was observing the Sprint when one of the racers, someone I knew, slipped and fell. She had to be carried off the track. As she passed me, our eyes met and I saw fear in hers, such awful fear; helplessness and hopelessness, too. I was powerless to help her and I thought my heart would break. I never saw her again. But I've never forgotten her. I never will. I don't want to forget her. Not ever. I don't want to forget any of my brothers and sisters. I want to remember each and every one of them. Forever. Shayna's lips trembled.

Another accident I won't forget happened at a track in Florida. While making one of those dangerous turns, a racer fell. He managed to get up, but must have become disoriented because he started to run in the wrong direction. He was too close to the electric rail and was electrocuted. But that wasn't all. The mechanical rabbit, which the racers are chasing, hit him. It hit him with such force that his chest exploded. It was horrible. His blood splattered everywhere. Everywhere. I cried. We all cried. I even saw tears in the eyes of some humans. And please, please don't tell me that dogs don't cry. We do. I tell you we do.

"Of course we do, Shayna. You're crying even now as you speak," said J.J.

As for that ice storm in November 1997, I don't know if any racers were injured. I can only assume some were. But if the dog racing industry really cared about us, as it says it does, racing would have been cancelled that night. It was wrong to force lean and muscled dogs who are so lacking in body fat to race under such dangerous conditions. Don't misunderstand. Greyhounds love to run. I'm nine and still run like the wind. Even though I stopped winning, I'm still a swift runner and hope to run until the day I die. However, it's one thing to run for fun and another to run for your life. But we have no choice. It's not up to us. We don't have the luxury of running for fun. Whenever we're running, we're truly running for our lives.

10 Fire

The industry says it cares about us, but that's all talk. Consider the kennel compound in Saugus, MA. That's where large numbers of racers from a Massachusetts track are housed. On Labor Day in 1992, a raging fire claimed the lives of many racers. The fire raged out of control because the compound is a firetrap. The buildings are constructed of wood and are very old. The cages are made of wood or wood and metal. Shredded paper lines the floors of the cages. And there's no automatic sprinkler system, which could have contained the fire. I know because I lived there while I raced at that particular track. I know because I was living there when the fire started. I know because I was among the lucky ones who were rescued.

But ninety-two others weren't so lucky. They perished. They burned to death. I heard their frantic cries. The fire fighters heard their cries too, but couldn't reach them in time. I was crying and so were they. One of them turned to me and said, "I'm so sorry we couldn't save everyone. I'm so very sorry." I rubbed my head against his leg. It was my way of saying I understood.

I was consumed with sadness. I felt no relief or joy in being alive. Ninety-two racing companions were dead. They burned to death. I couldn't even try to imagine their terror or their pain or their agony. A few I had known well. Others just slightly. Some I didn't know at all. But I cried for all of them. And I questioned why I was alive. Surely I wasn't more deserving than they. Why then was I among the living and they among the dead? For some questions there just aren't any answers.

"How did the fire start?" asked J.J.

"After a thorough investigation, it was determined that it was a case of arson," said Greta.

That doesn't surprise me, Greta. It wouldn't be the first time a fire was deliberately started. It's happened in stables and horses have perished.

"I know it has Shayna… By the way, did you know that the fire of 1992 wasn't the first?"

It wasn't?

"No. Few know this, but it was the third. The first was in 1986, when twenty-eight racers perished. The second was in 1990. It was described as a 'minor blaze' and fortunately no racers died. But it's just a matter of time before another fire claims the lives of more innocent dogs."

"What makes you say that?" asked Murphy.

"Because the compound was and still is a fire trap. The buildings were °renovated, but they're still made of wood, the cages are still made of wood or wood and metal, shredded paper still lines the floors the cages, and there still is no sprinkler system."

"Why not?" Murphy asked.

"Because no one, neither the track owner nor the owner of the kennel compound, wants to pay for the cost of installing a sprinkler system."

"This could be resolved if they shared the cost," offered Murphy.

"But apparently they won't," J.J. commented. "What does the state say? Shayna do you know?"

Yes, I know. The state says nothing. It stays out of it. Why? Because its primary concern is the revenue dog racing generates. It doesn't care that our pain and suffering are generating this revenue. It just doesn't care. As for the racing commission, I'm told it's supposed to protect us, but it seems to me that its primary concern is making certain that the tracks continue to generate revenue for the state. If this is so, then whenever a conflict arises between our safety and the state's revenue, we most likely don't stand a chance. We're even supposed to be grateful that some "No Smoking" signs are posted in the renovated compound.

You're right, Greta. It's just a matter of time before a fourth fire claims the lives of more innocent dogs. If a sprinkler system isn't installed, that compound should be condemned and closed. But of course, it won't be.

 We're Nobody's Property

"But aren't sprinkler systems required?" Murphy asked.

No, because according to the Massachusetts building code, kennels are treated like office buildings. And office buildings that are less than 12,000 square feet aren't required to have sprinkler systems. This is ok in the working environment of a regular office building, because people discover the fire and leave the building. This isn't the case with the residents of kennels, animal shelters and some animal hospitals because if the fire starts at night, when no humans are present and help arrives too late, the animals may either burn to death or die from smoke inhalation.

"But dogs aren't machines. We're not broken down appliances," said Murphy. "They don't bleed. We do. They don't suffer. We do. And we feel all the emotions that humans feel. We may be different from humans, but we're not less than humans."

You're right, Murphy, but the dog racing industry looks upon us as running machines, and running machines don't need sprinkler systems. If we burn to death in a fire, there are plenty of other racers waiting to take our places. It's the same when we stop winning by that second, or fraction of a second, and are discarded in much the same way broken refrigerators, TVs and other useless appliances and machines are discarded.

Yes, Murphy, you certainly are right. But being right doesn't count for much. It's power that counts. Humans crave power. Did you know there was a time when humans treated other humans like property, when men owned their wives and children and could do pretty much whatever they wanted with them? Think about it. Human women and children once were considered their husbands' and/or fathers' property! They no longer are. But we still are. And let's not forget about persons of color.

Do you remember the picture Greta showed us not long ago? It was a picture of black slaves working in the fields prior to the Civil War. They were wearing yokes around their necks and pulling heavy loads just like oxen are forced to do. This tells us that for hundreds of years white people viewed black people pretty much the same way they look upon us: as less than human. I'm glad humans no longer are enslaved in this country. I'm glad they're no longer anybody's property. I'm glad they're no longer forced to wear yokes around their necks. And I'm glad they're no longer bought and sold and beaten and murdered. But we still are.

I'm glad most human children no longer are torn out of their mother's arms. But our children still are. And the separation of parents from their children is painful regardless of species. How well I remember my pain and my mother's pain and sadness. We should not be bred and used and discarded like things. We need protection against the perverse acts of cruelty humans inflict upon us. Isn't it interesting that humans who have been brutalized by other humans say they were treated like animals? This clearly indicates that while brutalizing humans isn't acceptable, it's ok when the victims are other-than-humans.

Black slaves committed no crime, unless having a dark complexion is a crime. As for us, our only crime is being a second (or less) too slow on the track. Black humans were once looked upon as sub-humans. We still are. They said black humans lacked souls. They say the same about us.

"They said the same about the Jews of Europe and the former Soviet Union," commented Greta. "For about a decade, starting in the mid 1930s and lasting until the Nazis were defeated in 1945, Jews were treated like animals of other species. They were rounded up and packed in railroad cars, as are animals of other species. They were transported with no food, water or rest stops to death camps, another name for human slaughterhouses, as are animals of other species. Under Nazi law, Jews were considered *unter-menchen*, which means less-than-human. Killing them was legal and done on a mammoth scale. It was murder made legal by law."

"As is hunting, eating and experimenting on animals," commented J.J.

"As was the murder of six million Jews, among them one-and-a-half million children," said Greta. "Their crime? They were Jewish. The Greyhounds' crime? Being seconds or a fraction of a second too slow on the track."

"Here's something interesting to think about," said J.J. "Humans who have political power have the power of life and death over animals of other species and some humans. Those who have no political power still have the power of life and death over us. Then there are the exploited and impoverished humans who are abused and treated like second-class citizens. They too have the power of life and death over us. Instead of feeling connected to us in some small way, they also use and abuse us; perhaps not all, but some do."

"No one should have that kind of power over anyone and we shouldn't be at the mercy of humans who decide whether we live or die."

You're right, Murphy. I never mentioned this before, but sometimes I wish I had been born a human with political power because I'd use it to help all innocent and oppressed animals everywhere, both other-specied animals and human animals. And there's something else. Sometimes I think I believe that somewhere inside human animals there's a soft voice telling them that slavery is wrong. But many don't listen to this voice, which happens to be their conscience. They dare not listen because listening means they'll have to start rethinking about what's right and wrong. And doing that might just persuade them that enslaving anyone, regardless of species, is wrong. It could turn their entire world upside down.

But the Abolitionists listened. They listened to their conscience, acted on it and, as a result, their lives were changed forever. They were beaten and terrorized. Some were murdered. It's not easy being part of an idea that's ahead of its time. And it isn't always easy to listen to your conscience. But the Abolitionists of the 1800s did listen. They listened and decided that the idea behind human rights was that all humans, regardless of color, have rights simply because they're humans.

Today's Abolitionists are taking this idea a step further. They've been listening to their conscience and believe that rights shouldn't be reserved exclusively for humans. They understand that all living beings, regardless of species, have the right to live and the right to feel and be safe. They understand that we need our own Bill of Rights and they're willing to act as our advocates. They're willing to protect us and help enforce our rights. These are good people. Decent people.

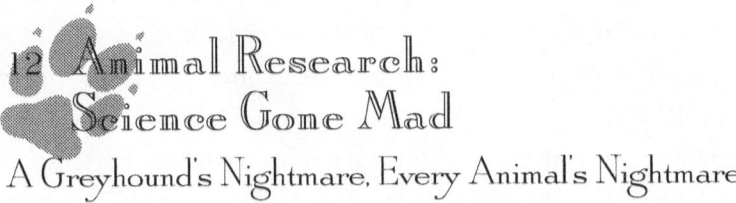

12 Animal Research:
Science Gone Mad
A Greyhound's Nightmare, Every Animal's Nightmare

"While I was incarcerated in a shelter, there was talk that each year millions of homeless dogs – cats, too – were being put to death in shelters throughout the country. Are retired racers competing with shelter dogs for the same scarce homes?" asked Murphy.

Yes we are. But it's not our fault. The fault lies with the dog racing industry for bringing so many of us into the world and then discarding us once we're considered unprofitable and no longer useful. This contributes to the terrible toll on shelters nationwide.

"I remember a racer who was brought to the shelter where I was incarcerated. I still don't understand why I was incarcerated and confined to a cage. I'd done nothing wrong. None of us had done anything wrong. We'd committed no crime; unless it's a crime to be homeless. It seems to me, though, that the real criminals are the persons who breed us, abuse and neglect us, then abandon us or surrender us to a shelter. But getting back to the racer, I remember him well.

"His name was Big Boy, and when he arrived he was so infested with fleas and ticks that he required many medicated baths to get rid of them. He also had bald spots on his hind-quarters, which he said came from the constant rubbing of his body against the sides of the small metal cage to which he had been confined most of the day. Twenty or more hours a day, he said. He was one of about sixty retired racers who were to be sold to a university research laboratory. He told me that researchers like to use former racers because they have gentle dispositions and are accustomed to being handled by humans. In addition, they have large chests and researchers like to use them in chest surgery experiments. I suppose that's the price racers must pay for having a gentle disposition and a body that was made for running."

"And being looked down upon as somebody's property," commented J.J.

"Fortunately, Big Boy got a temporary reprieve because the university decided it needed only fifty racers, not sixty. He didn't know what became of the other nine racers, but I remember clearly that he trembled whenever he spoke about the fifty racers who had been sold for research purposes. He said being experimented on was the worst thing that could happen to anyone.

"Big Boy had a name for the researchers. He called them 'the killers in white coats.' He said they experiment on racers over and over and over again before they finally kill them and end their pain and suffering. He said racers are especially vulnerable whenever a track closes, whether for good or until the next season, because at such times many are retired and have to go somewhere. Sometimes the adoption groups are filled to capacity.

"Then there's the question of money. Big Boy explained that placing racers with adoption groups doesn't bring in any money, whereas selling them for research purposes does. So it's not an uncommon practice for trainers and breeders to sell retired racers to university and government laboratories. According to Big Boy, the American Greyhound Racing Association doesn't try to stop these sales. In fact, it has no problem with them so long as they're done with the knowledge and consent of the dogs' *owners* of record.

"I liked Big Boy. One day a woman and young boy visited the shelter. They liked him too. They liked me, but they liked him more and adopted him. I was disappointed, but Big Boy deserved a break. Life on the track is hard. Very hard. I remember his broken tail. It broke at a track where he was racing when the door of the starting box closed on it at the beginning of a race. He said he was in terrible pain, but he raced anyway and finished in fourth place. But fourth place isn't good enough. Especially for a Grade C racer. That's why he was scheduled to go to a research lab. Big Boy needed a break. He really needed a break. What's more, he deserved one."

"But your life wasn't easy and you deserved a break too," commented J.J.

"I got my break a few days later when Greta visited the shelter and brought me home with her. It's a good thing she did, because my time was running out. A lethal injection was in store for me. I know it's painless, but I didn't want to die. I was only two years old and I wanted to live. None of the other shelter residents wanted to die either. Humans call it euthanasia, but it's not. It's murder. Whenever a homeless animal is put to death because there's no room at the shelter, it's a case of murder. I know all the rationalizations. I know them by heart. But it's murder whenever a living being is put to death just because he or she is homeless."

"You're right, Murphy. And so was Big Boy," said Greta. "Last night I read another article about Greyhounds being used for research purposes. For years trainers have been selling retired racers to university schools of veterinary medicine. Within the last three years, one of them bought more than 2,600 racers from local trainers and breeders. Think about it. In just three years one school bought, used and killed more than 2,600 former racers.

"Many were killed to teach surgical procedures to students; spaying and neutering, for instance. Greyhounds were deliberately killed so that students could learn how to spay and neuter living dogs! Others were killed in order to teach dental procedures to vet students. They were taught how to clean dogs' teeth using the severed heads of racers! Greyhounds actually were killed and decapitated so that students could use their heads to learn how to clean the teeth of living dogs! This is an outrage!" There was a moment of silence.

"Heartless and cruel too," said Murphy. "And senseless because future veterinarians will be cleaning the teeth of living dogs, not dead dogs. And they'll be spaying and neutering living dogs, not dead dogs. If they must work on dead dogs, they should use dogs who have died in accidents and from disease."

"You're right, Murphy," said J.J. "Everyone knows you don't have to use and then kill living beings in order to teach anyone anything. Especially today when computer-based models, videos, sophisticated dummies and other technologies are available. And veterinary students can learn so much by observing veterinarians operating on animals who need surgery. If I know this, and I didn't go to high school or college, then the killers in the white coats know it, too."

"Of course they know," said Greta. "But animal research is a multimillion dollar industry. That's why, in just one year – I believe it was 1997 – this same veterinary medical school experimented on and then killed almost a thousand former racers. But before their bodies were cremated, some of their organs were removed and sent to an elementary school."

"What?" asked J.J., Murphy and Shayna in unison. "What for?"

"For dissection purposes. To give fifth grade students an opportunity to dissect the brains, hearts and eyeballs of former racers. The children poked at them like they were toys or other objets that had been purchased in a specialty shop. Their remarks were quite callous, and no mention was made of the organs' original owners, the gentle Greyhounds."

"Dissection is unconscionable," said Murphy. "It's cruel and destructive and it's damaging children by destroying their sensitivity and reverence for life, all life. It's also reinforcing the idea that we're just things that can be used and then discarded in whichever way humans decide. Shayna is right. We need a Bill of Rights of our own."

"According to the same article," Greta continued, "Big Boy was right in another way, too. The university paid $120 for each racer, whereas it would have had to pay $400 for a specially-bred laboratory dog. Multiply this $280 difference by a few thousand dogs and you'll see that the university is saving a huge amount of money. At the same time, those who sold them the racers received $120 for each racer instead of donating them – for free – to an adoption group. They also saved the cost of paying for lethal injections, which must be administered by a veterinarian or trained technician. Because sale to laboratories is profitable for both buyers and sellers, breeders and trainers of some of the country's fastest dogs have been participating in this heinous practice. In fact, these persons reportedly are quite well-known and respected throughout the dog racing industry."

Can't something be done to stop this? asked Shayna.

"Probably not, because the American Greyhound Racing Association, which is the national organization, doesn't oppose it and won't take a firm position against it. In addition, the National Greyhound Advisory Council, which was created by the national organization, passed a resolution discouraging, but not prohibiting the sale or donation of racers to research facilities. The Council was created to improve the industry's image. To accomplish this, it was entrusted with humane issues as they affect racers. But it doesn't appear to be interested in saving lives. In fact, it's been reported that one of its members sold one or more of his racers to the aforementioned veterinary school!

"At one time some of these racers earned huge amounts of money for their humans but, as big Boy said, for $120 they turned them over to the 'killers in white coats.' Among them were nine- and ten-year-old females who were first used for racing and then breeding, and whose children and grandchildren won many Titles and large sums of money for these ungrateful people."

All eyes turned to Shayna. Had this been the fate of the mother she loved so dearly? Shayna didn't say a word, but it was obvious that she was thinking about her mother.

"Very young puppies were among the victims, as were older dogs. No age group was excluded, although the vast majority were in the two-year-old range."

"Greta, doesn't loyalty count for anything?" Murphy asked.

Loyalty? We're considered property, Murphy. No one feels loyalty for a piece of property.

"You're right Shayna," continued Greta. "Furthermore, loyalty isn't something the industry understands. As Big Boy explained to Murphy, selling retired racers to research laboratories is acceptable to the industry so long as it's done with the knowledge and consent of their legal *owners*."

Greta, please don't use that word. Nobody *owns* us.

"Oh yes they do, Shayna. What you mean is nobody should own us," said J.J.

"I'm afraid J.J. is right, Shayna."

I understand what you and J.J. are saying, Greta, so now let's make it clear that whenever we use the words "*own*" and "*owners*" we're doing so for purposes of clarity only, because living beings shouldn't and mustn't be owned.

"I agree, Shayna. As I was saying, the industry says it's ok to sell retired racers to research labs provided their *owners* of record gave their consent. But because some people buy Greyhounds as investments and then lease them to kennel operators and trainers in other states, they often have no contact either with the dogs or the persons who leased them. That being the case, those who leased the dogs usually have total control over them and can do pretty much whatever they want with them."

"As did slave *owners* with respect to their slaves," commented Murphy.

"That's right Murphy, but when there's an exposé and *owners* learn that their racers were sent to research laboratories without their permission," problems arise. In this case, some *owners* were told that their dogs had been placed for adoption once they stopped winning. They didn't know they had been sold for research purposes.

"Some were shocked and angry for the right reasons; others because it was done without their permission. I'm afraid more were angry for the wrong reasons. In fact, it was reported that a state official said the issue wasn't with the university for having bought the racers; it was about *owners* having the right to know what happens to their property. And the dean of the veterinary school said he didn't understand what all the fuss was about since the racers would have been killed anyway by other painful methods.

"This wasn't an isolated incident. Between 1996 and 1998, the four dog tracks in Alabama reportedly donated or sold more than 250 racers to a university's veterinary medical school, the vast majority without their *owners'* knowledge or consent. Some *owners* were quite upset. One of them was lucky because her dog was still alive and she was able to retrieve him. But most of the dogs were already dead.

"Once again age wasn't a factor. Included were youngsters under two and seniors of eleven. A spokesperson for the university said it had assumed that the persons who released the racers to them had the authority to do so. He said that in the future the university would be more careful. The public was outraged, yet retired racers continue to be sold and used for research purposes. And you can be pretty certain that whenever they're donated instead of sold, they're claimed as valuable income tax deductions."

"This is what can and does happen to you when you're classified as property. Anyone's property."

"Yes, Murphy, but Greyhounds aren't the only animals who are used for research purposes," Greta explained. "Mice and rats, guinea pigs and rabbits, dogs and cats, cows and horses, monkeys, chimpanzees and other non-human primates are researchers' favorite tools. Human primates, too. In the Nazi death camps, persons of the Jewish faith were used in a variety of barbaric and painful experiments. The ones who managed to survive carry the physical and emotional scars for the remainder of their lives."

Three pairs of eyes focused lovingly on Greta, who is of the Jewish faith. "I was first introduced to animal research and its horrors by a large national organization," said Greta. "That was many, many years ago, but the pictures of terrified monkeys restrained in stereotaxic devices will remain with me forever. I remember hoping this information wasn't true. But it was. It is.

"Animal testing isn't just cruel," Greta continued. "It's time consuming and expensive as well. It costs taxpayers hundreds of millions of dollars each year and in addition, it's misleading because drugs and chemicals that test safe on animals of other species often are harmful to humans. For example, sheep tolerate strychnine, which is deadly to humans; penicillin kills guinea pigs; cats can't tolerate aspirin and thalidomide, which tested safe on pregnant rabbits, caused severe and tragic birth defects in humans.

"Animal tests only tell us what will happen to the laboratory animals who are exposed to certain drugs and chemicals. They don't tell us how human animals will react to them. For this reason I believe testing cosmetics on lab animals recently was banned in Great Britain, and I believe they're considering banning medical experiments as well. This will save many lives because money that once was used for animal research will be available for disease prevention programs and for high tech research that doesn't use animals of other species."

"Torturing and murdering one group of living beings for the supposed benefit of another group doesn't work. It just doesn't work," commented J.J. "It's science gone evil."

"You're right, J.J.," said Murphy. "Furthermore, torturing and murdering us in the name of science doesn't help or cure humans. We're too different."

"Then why do they do it?" asked J.J.

"Because animal research is a multi-million dollar industry," explained Greta. "The companies that profit from it include the makers and sellers of laboratory equipment such as surgical and dissection tables, restraining devices and other instruments of torture that are used in research laboratories. Likewise pharmaceutical companies that make and market the chemicals and drugs which researchers infuse into lab animals; they profit enormously. And then there are the companies that breed the laboratory animals, many of whom are primates. Other primates are captured in the wild and exported to research laboratories world-wide, including the United States."

Don't forget the researchers, Greta. The federal government gives them millions of dollars in grants each year.

"It does, Shayna. I've even heard that at one university in Massachusetts, about 1,500 primates are enslaved and used in painful and terminal experiments. Some of the things they do to them in the name of science are beyond understanding. Animal experimentation isn't just science gone evil. It's science gone mad."

"You've mentioned primates a few times, Greta. Just what are they?" asked J.J.

"They're a family of animals that has some characteristics in common. For instance, they can walk upright on two legs. There are two categories of primates: human and non-human. People are human primates. Some of the non-human primates include monkeys, chimpanzees, orangutans, baboons, bonobos and gorillas. Few know this but, genetically speaking, chimpanzees and humans are more than 98% identical. But that less than 2% difference makes them invalid research models for humans. Nevertheless, researchers at large universities are paid huge sums of money to conduct a variety of experiments on them and other animals.

"Addiction experiments for instance. Unlike humans, other-specied animals must be forced to become addicted to heroin, cocaine, amphetamines, nicotine and alcohol. Only sick and twisted minds would force these animals to become addicts under the pretense of helping humans. Force-feeding these drugs to primates and other-specied animals causes them to suffer hallucinations, depression, self-mutilation, seizures and more. And while taxpayer dollars are being wasted to fund this senseless research, human addicts are suffering because drug treatment programs have been shut down or cut back because of a lack of funds."

But even if non-human primates and other animals were valid research models for humans, it still would be wrong to use them to benefit humans. Animal research is the enslavement of the defenseless and weak by the powerful and strong.

"I agree with you, Shayna. And I believe that while humans continue to use, abuse and murder other animals for whatever reasons, they'll continue to do the same to each other. Not many persons are aware of this, but in the United Sates humans have been subjected to a variety of experiments without their consent and some-times without their knowledge."

"Without knowing they were being used in experiments?"

"That's right, Murphy. For instance, it's been reported that American military personnel have been subjected to radiation experiments without their knowledge or consent and with dire consequences. It's also been reported that poor and powerless adults and children, who are wards of the state and have no advocates to protect and speak for them, have been subjected to a variety of experiments."

"And nobody objects?" J.J. was incredulous.

"It hasn't been publicized, so few are aware," explained Greta.

"Big Boy called the researchers killers in white coats because it was while wearing those white coats that they experimented on and murdered innocent creatures. Yet when these persons remove their white coats and leave their laboratories, they melt into the crowd and appear like everyone else," Murphy commented.

"But they're not like everyone else," said J.J. "They inflict pain, suffering and death on the innocent."

But they can change, said Shayna. Some have. Some vivisectors have stopped experimenting on us because they finally realized that animal research is ethically and scientifically wrong. Some have even become outspoken foes of animal research.

The killing must stop. Soon we'll be entering the 21st century and the killing must stop! Physicians and scientists who experiment on us for whatever reasons are violating an important rule of medicine that says, First Do No Harm. I know I've said this before, but I'm going to say it again. I don't understand humans. I don't understand the human species. I don't understand the human mentality. Shayna was silent for a moment, then she continued.

I've mentioned this before, but it too bears repeating. While human slavery was legal in the U.S., slave *owners* did whatever they wanted to their slaves. They beat them. Often they beat them to death. They hanged them. They skinned them while they were still alive. It was ok to do this. It was ok and it was legal because the slaves were property. But it wasn't ok if someone else harmed them without their *owner's* consent. Whenever that happened, slave *owners* could sue those persons in a court of law for compensation for damaging their property.

"It took a Civil War to put an end to human slavery in the U.S. It was a war that destroyed many lives and almost destroyed the country," said Greta.

But our enslavement continues; we're still at the mercy of persons who use, abuse and then dispose of us in any which awful way. Murphy, you seem pensive. Is there something else you wish to say?

"Yes Shayna, there is. I can't stop thinking about the methods humans use to torture and murder other-specied animals. They breed them and raise them in order to eat them and wear them. They hunt them for the thrill of the kill. Yes, the thrill of the kill. They experiment on them senselessly and sadistically, and brutalize them in so-called sport and entertainment."

And then there are the beavers. It breaks my heart whenever I think about those intelligent architects who drown in underwater traps that are set by humans.

"Yes, Shayna, it is heartbreaking. And I've heard that these intelligent architects die slowly and painfully in those underwater traps. I believe it can take as long as twenty minutes. No offense meant Greta, but I believe the human species is a species gone mad."

"No offense taken, Murphy," said Greta. "I think I agree with you."

 13 The United States/South American Connection

"My mom told me," said J.J., "that racers have been sold to tracks in other countries and with disastrous results. During some of our quiet talks together she told me a lot about dog racing. She was relieved that I wasn't a racer, but worried about her children who were. I think about them, my siblings, and my father too. I wonder about all of them. What happened to them? Are they all right? Perhaps I really don't want to know. I do know, however, that I'm a lucky Greyhound. I'm lucky because I never had to race and because I had such a wonderful mother.

"She was special. Very special and it hurt so much when she died. When she died I lost my best friend. Some believe the steroids as well as the poor nutrition she received at the track hastened her death. She told me about the cheap, diseased raw meat she and other racers were fed. Like you said Shayna, it smelled and tasted bad, but she and the other racers ate it because they were hungry. And you're right, Shayna, with good care and nutrition Greyhounds can live thirteen, fourteen or fifteen years. But not many retired racers live that long.

"During our quiet talks together, mom would tell me about the hard lives racers lived. She'd say that winners live and losers die, but sooner or later everyone loses. No one, she said, can remain a winner forever. Sometimes she'd see a bumper sticker on a car that read, Greyhounds: First They Run, Then They Die. 'That's true,' she'd say, 'deadly true.' Then, our adoptive mother bought one of those bumper stickers and after she pasted it on the bumper of her van, mom just wouldn't stop licking and kissing her.

"One day, after mom stopped winning at the track, her trainer told her he planned to send her to a country in South America where a dog track was being constructed. He told her he was doing the right thing because his only other option was to put her to death. Were the adoption groups filled to capacity, she wondered? Had he inquired? She didn't know. She did know that she didn't want to go to South America because she'd heard that conditions there were even worse than here. On the other hand, she didn't want to be put to death. But because she was somebody's property, she had no control over her own life. Fortunately, she never left the U.S. because it was discovered that she was pregnant. As it turned out, that was her lucky break.

"Mom's fears were justified because a few years later, hundreds of American racers were found dead and dying at an abandoned and bankrupt dog track in Venezuela. They came from various parts of the U.S., including here in New England. And the year before, two hundred American racers, who were waiting to be transported to Venezuela, were found starving to death at a Greyhound farm in Florida. Neither of these tragedies made the headlines. They rarely do."

"Mexico is another Greyhound hell," said Greta. "Some years ago the owner of a dog track there admitted on American TV that he fed his slow American racers to his cheetahs. I don't know if he killed them first or if the cheetahs killed them and then ate them."

Oh Greta, there's no end to the horror stories.

"I'm afraid you're right, Shayna. The Irish sell racers to dog tracks in Spain and when their racing careers are over, many are sold to hunters. When the hunters have no more use for them they dispose of them by hanging. I've read that if they were good hunting dogs, they're hanged in a manner that kills them quickly. And if they weren't, they're hanged in a manner that causes them to die slowly and in great agony."

Silence.

"As for Ireland, it's been reported that unprofitable racers are sometimes drowned," Greta continued. "Others are killed outright or abandoned and left to starve to death. There's also been talk that in some countries racers are eaten. You're right, Shayna, there's no end to the horror.

"And because dog racing appears to be dying in the U.S., the industry is trying to bring it into other countries. Vietnam, for example.

"Do you think they will?" asked J.J.

"I don't know, but they're certainly trying."

14 Death by Electrocution

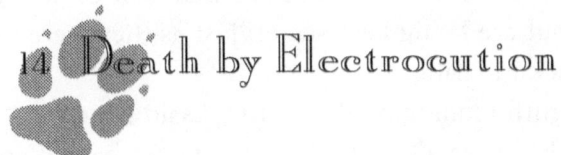

For years the shocking truth about young racers being slowly and painfully electrocuted at a dog track in Idaho was a well-kept secret.

"My mom told me about that track," said J.J. "She said it was an end-of-the-line dog track where some of the slowest Greyhounds raced."

Careful, J.J. Remember that "slow" means losing by a second or just a fraction of a second. There are no slow racers...

"I know there aren't, Shayna. And I meant no offense."

I know you didn't, J.J. I'm just pretty sensitive when it comes to racers and former racers.

"My mom told me that back in 1993, a local reporter described not just electrocutions, but shootings, fatal beatings and throat slashings at this track. Yet, no action was taken. The reporter advised that the national organization and the state racing commission had been made aware of these atrocities."

The track finally did close, J.J. It closed as a result of another exposé in 1995, after witnesses testified about these atrocities. One said he witnessed the electrocutions. Another said he saw a trainer beat puppies to death with a claw hammer. Some trainers admitted to administering drugs to racers in order to determine the outcome of races. Now dog racing is illegal in Idaho.

"But first untold numbers of innocents had to suffer and die in agony," said J.J. He was visibly shaken and Shayna paused for a moment before continuing.

This form of electrocution is known as the Tijuana Hot Plate because it originated at a dog track in Tijuana, Mexico. The name itself is enough to send shivers up and down your spine. It's a slow and painful form of murder. Cheap, too. I won't describe how it's done, but the dogs scream and cry in agony for about thirty seconds before they die. Shayna's voice was unsteady.

It frightens and upsets me that electrocutions may still be in use elsewhere in the U.S., but are being kept secret, just as they were for so many years at the track in Idaho.

"And those other frightful killing methods, too," said Murphy.

"It's certainly possible. After all, it took two exposés before any action was taken at the Idaho track," commented J.J.

"There are many dog tracks operating in the U.S.," explained Greta. "At last count there were forty-eight operating in fifteen states, with an average of about a thousand racers at each track. That's a huge operation, so huge the national organization can't possibly be aware of all the atrocities taking place. Dog racing isn't just a huge national operation; it's international as well. Racers are constantly being transported from one state to another as well as to other countries. That's the nature of dog racing. So even if it wanted to, the national organization couldn't possibly control such a huge and dispersed operation. And that's why state laws, no matter how well-intentioned, can't protect these gentle dogs. Whenever they race and wherever they race, whether in the U.S. or elsewhere, Greyhound racers are always at risk.

15 Once Life was Good
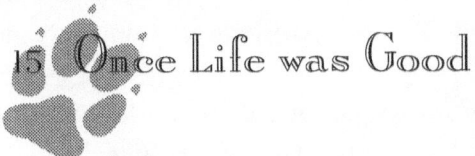

We weren't always treated so cruelly. Once life was good. Few persons know this, but Greyhounds are probably the oldest purebred breed of dog. I believe we're the only dog mentioned in the Old Testament and we lived as long ago as 6000 BC in an area that is now Turkey. Thousands of years ago the pharaohs of Egypt revered us, so much that only royalty were permitted to keep us. Ordinary persons could not. It also was a crime, indeed a capital crime, to harm us. The Ancient Greeks and Romans revered us too, and the goddess Diana is always shown with a Greyhound at her side. We were Alexander the Great's favorite dog, and we witnessed the rise and fall of Ancient Greece and Rome.

"Why were you so revered?" asked Murphy.

We were revered for our grace, our speed and our intelligence. And because we were carefully protected, we raced for thousands of years without ever coming to harm.

"Then what happened?" asked Murphy.

Dog racing for profit started in the late 19th and early 20th centuries, and ever since then we've been murdered instead of revered. In fact, in dog racing's seventy-two-year history in the U.S., about a million racers have lost their lives. How ironic that our speed and grace, our bodies that were built to run, our gentle dispositions and our intelligence should lead to our pain and suffering. We love to run. In fact, running for fun and snuggling at the side of someone we love are the things we love to do most.

The one thing we don't want to do is run for our lives. I believe it's been estimated that more than 20,000 racers are murdered each year in the U.S., many by cheap and painful methods. I don't know what the toll is in other countries. But, as Greta pointed out, in Spain racers are hanged and in Ireland they're abandoned to starve to death or drowned. There's talk that in some places they're eaten. It's not good. Dog racing is not good. Wherever it's active, things are not good. They're just not good.

"My mom said if humans want to gamble, there are lots of other gambling options. They don't have to bet on living beings."

Your mom was a smart dog, J.J.

"She was more than smart. She was gentle, very gentle, and so very loving. I suppose that's why I can't understand the human capacity for cruelty. Sometimes I think it might even be a form of madness because intelligent persons, persons who are respected in their communities and who hold responsible jobs engage in horrendous acts of cruelty. If it's not a form of madness, then what is it?"

"I've asked myself that question many times, J.J.," said Greta, "and I don't have the answer. Perhaps it's a genetic defect. Perhaps humans lack the gene that triggers compassion. I don't know, but there are times when I wish I could get a divorce from the human species."

"You wouldn't want to do that," said Murphy.

"Sometimes I think I would."

"But you'd be powerless, like us. And then you wouldn't be able to help us."

"I suppose you're right, Murphy. But sometimes I think there must be a gene for compassion, which large numbers of humans do lack. Rousseau wouldn't agree. He said cruelty is learned. He said people are born good and learn cruelty while being socialized. But I don't know. I just don't know..."

Well, I know this, Greta: Greyhounds don't want to be revered. We don't need to be revered. But we don't want to be brutalized either. We don't want to be bred to die. We don't want to be raced and then discarded like broken machines. Because we're not machines. We're dogs. We're members of a different species, but not a lesser one. And we want to be treated as such. We want to live in peace with humans, but that won't be possible until humans start treating us like living beings who have our own intrinsic value regardless of how useful we are (or aren't) to them.

This means that dog racing must become a thing of the past, as must all forms of so-called sport and entertainment that use and abuse us, and others. All it would take is compassion. Humans underestimate the power of compassion, but it's a lot more powerful than they imagine. And they shouldn't be ashamed of it either. In fact, they should start looking for it because I believe it lies somewhere deep inside them. I'm pretty sure it does. They just don't know it.

"Or they may not feel comfortable acknowledging it," said Murphy. "Perhaps they're ashamed to acknowledge it. For some strange reason, many humans believe that gentleness and compassion are signs of weakness. But just the opposite is true. Gentleness and compassion are not signs of weakness but of true strength."

"How eloquent you both are," said J.J., and his eyes expressed the admiration and deep feelings he felt for his two close friends.

16 It's Safer to Be a Legislator Than a Racer

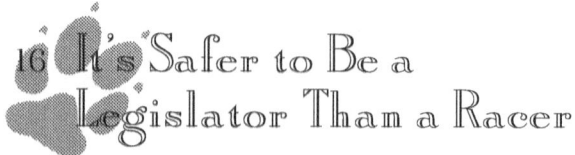

In spite of my wonderful family, there are still days when I feel depressed and can't stop crying. Humans call days like these their "dog" days. Hmmm … how interesting. Fortunately, my family understands my sadness, and their love and support help me get through my own dog days. So does knowing there are lots of good people out there who care, and that bills were filed that would have made dog racing illegal in Massachusetts.

In December 1994, a young and courageous state representative filed a bill to end dog racing in Massachusetts. It was the first such bill filed in a state where dog racing was active and legal. It died in a study committee in the summer of 1996. In December of that year, he filed a similar bill, which also died in a study committee two years after the first.

Why did they die? At first, the committee responsible for the bills cited state revenue as an excuse. When reminded that the amount of revenue generated by dog racing had declined drastically in the last ten years and was just a fraction of one percent of total state revenue, committee members used jobs as an excuse for not giving either bill a favorable report. But I believe it's been estimated that the number of jobs at risk is under a thousand, the vast majority of which are part-time, low paying jobs that don't include benefits. These persons could be trained for jobs that would pay decent livable wages, including benefits, and would do no harm – no harm to anyone.

I remember Greta traveling to the State House in Boston in 1995 and again in 1997, to testify on behalf of these bills at public hearings before this committee. The shelter manager of a humane society also testified. He testified that one of his duties was to put racers to death at the request of their trainers. Many came from a dog track in

Vermont and it's pretty certain that at least some of them once raced in Massachusetts.

He said he didn't like killing them, but for a few years he thought it was better for them to die painlessly at the hands of someone who cared about them instead of painfully and violently by a hammer or other instrument. Those were his words. He testified that the dogs were just entering the prime of their lives, but because they were just seconds too slow on the track, their trainers/*owners* made it clear they wanted them killed so that they could race other dogs.

"If they didn't breed so many racers they wouldn't be so fast to kill them," said Murphy. "I know I'm repeating myself, but over-breeding goes hand in hand with killing. It's responsible for the large numbers of youngsters waiting to start their racing careers who then are discarded when they stop winning. It's a cruel and ugly cycle that repeats itself over and over and over again."

That's right, Murphy. It's the over-breeding that makes racers discardable and expendable. Greta, do you have a copy of the shelter manager's testimony?

"Yes I do. In his testimony, he told the committee, 'I saw wounds, gashes, infections and broken legs that were left untreated. I saw dehydration, starvation, infestation of parasites, anemia and torn ears and flesh from track accidents and fights. Finally, in August of 1992, I could not take it any longer. I had received twelve dogs from an *owner*, only to find five dogs in deplorable condition. I had to take a stand, not just for the five Greyhounds in question, but for the 1,200 plus other Greyhounds who never had a chance.'"

"What does he mean by the 1,200 plus other greyhounds who never had a chance?" asked J.J.

"He's talking about the more than 1,200 racers he put to death in a five-year period, racers who were seconds or fractions of a second too slow on the track. He said sometimes trainers stopped feeding the dogs when they stopped winning and earning their own keep. He said he turned all the evidence over to a humane society in Vermont and believes it helped end dog racing in Vermont."

"What kind of evidence was he talking about?" asked Murphy.

"His own recorded observations over that five-year period as well as some graphic photos he took of starved and emaciated racers, and racers with horrible bruises on their bodies. On the other hand, some looked well-nourished and healthy. None of them should have died. Not one. After a thorough investigation and a good deal of local publicity, the track closed in late 1992. Three years later, a law was passed making dog racing illegal in Vermont. It was named after the Greyhound who inspired it. But dog racing is still legal in Massachusetts and fourteen other states in the U.S. In many other countries, too."

Yet in spite of this compelling testimony, in spite of the photos of bruised and starved racers that were submitted, in spite of the convincing testimony given by many other persons at the two public hearings, the committee members refused to give either bill a favorable report. They probably feared they'd be putting their political careers at risk if they did.

Since neither bill was reported out of committee favorably, the House and Senate never had the opportunity to consider, debate or vote on them. Yet the committee received a tremendous amount of mail in support of both. Regarding the first bill, I've heard that it has a file almost a foot thick with mail in favor of abolition. Surely this demonstrates the wide gap that exists between the will of the people and the will of their legislators.

Politicians are luckier than we are. When they lose an election they don't lose their lives. Nobody calls them losers, and they go on with their lives and continue to be respected. That's not the case with us. Whenever we race, our lives are at risk. Whenever we lose a few races in each grade by just a second or less, we're in danger of losing not just our careers, but our lives as well. While we continue to win, we're safe. Once we stop winning, most of us are doomed.

This should not be! Nobody can remain a winner forever! Like politicians and other humans who compete against each other in sports, theatre and the arts, our lives also have value and meaning after we stop winning. They do. I know they do. And no one can tell me otherwise.

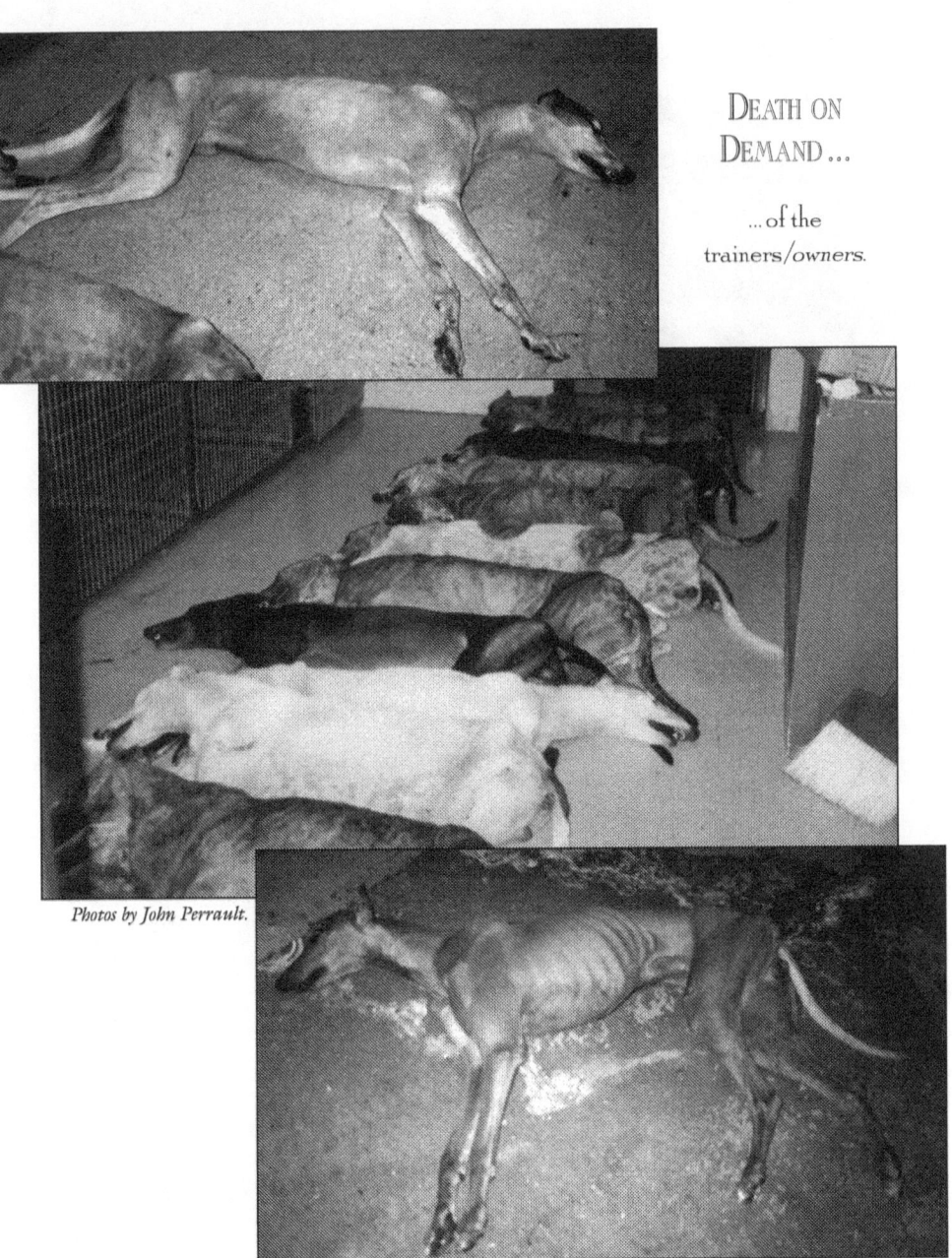

DEATH ON
DEMAND...

...of the
trainers/owners.

Photos by John Perrault.

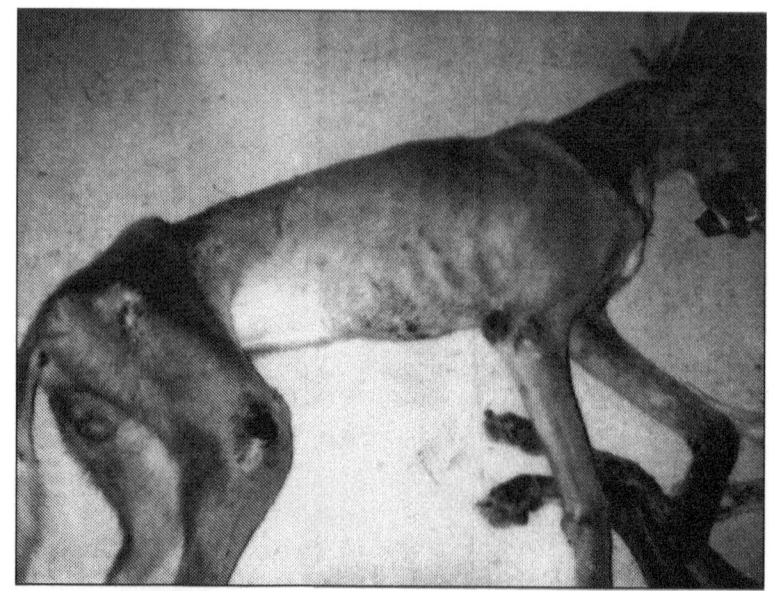

Photos by John Perrault.

MORE DEATH
ON DEMAND.

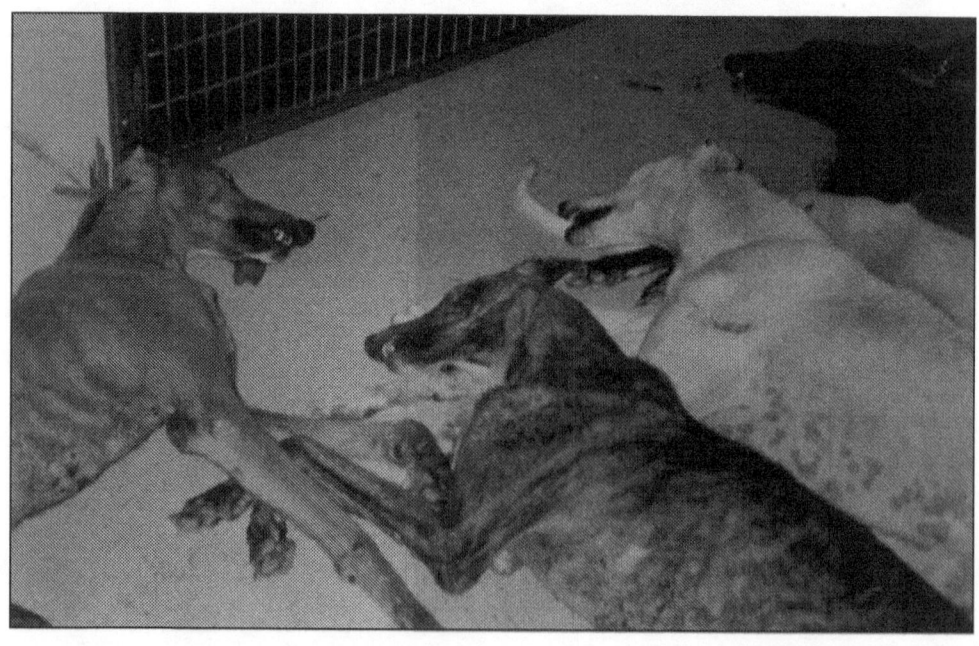

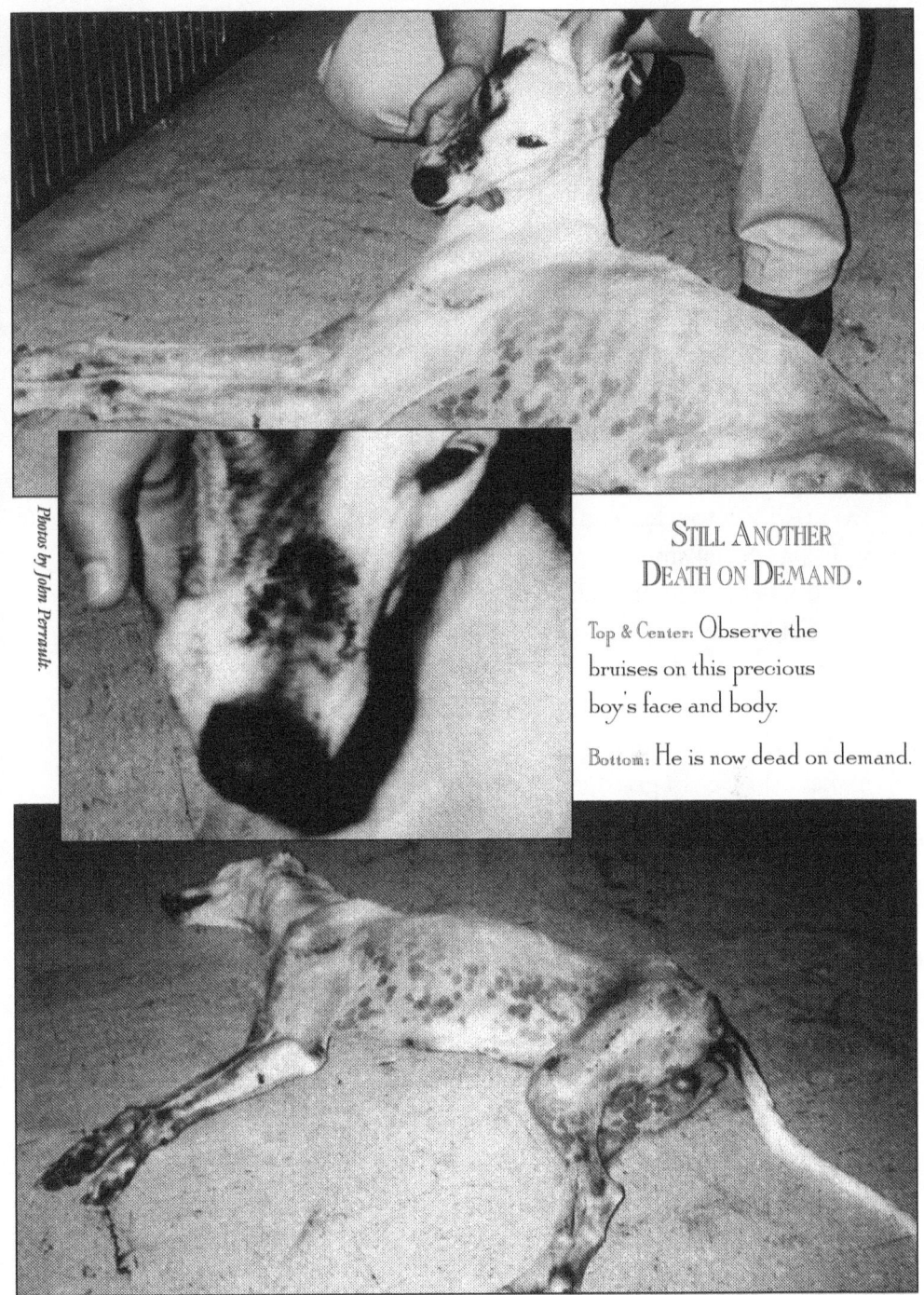

Photos by John Perrault.

STILL ANOTHER
DEATH ON DEMAND .

Top & Center: Observe the
bruises on this precious
boy's face and body.

Bottom: He is now dead on demand.

 17 Love and Hugs and Kisses

Six years have passed since I came to live with Murphy and Greta and their barn friends, who became my friends, too. Those six years passed very fast. I remember learning how to sit. Imagine that! I was four years old and had to learn how to sit! That's because racers aren't permitted to sit. We may stand or lie down, but sitting isn't permitted. So I had to unlearn previous training in order to learn how to sit. It wasn't easy. Greta and I attended training classes and the trainer and other dogs, who took sitting for granted, were so patient. Eventually I too learned, and now whenever Greta sees me sit, she smiles a special smile and I smile back.

I learned to climb stairs, too. That was easy. And I learned about love. That was the easiest of all. It's such a nice feeling, being loved. I remember being loved a long time ago by my mother when I was a very young puppy. And I remember how wonderful it felt to love her back. Loving is something you never forget. To love and be loved makes you feel so good, so warm and safe. And it feels so good to be touched gently and to be kissed. Hugged, too. And whenever someone hugs me I remember Anna, the animal control officer who gave me my very first hug when I was almost four years old. She's the person who made it possible for me to start my brand new life. I'll never forget her. I'll always remember her with love and gratitude.

Yes, it certainly is wonderful to be loved and to have someone to love back. Like compassion, love is powerful stuff. It could heal the world if people would just let it. But first they will have to stop fearing and looking down upon other beings who are different from them. They'll have to stop looking down upon animals of other species and some members of their own species as lesser beings and mere commodities. In addition, they'll have to stop looking down upon other-specied animals as trophies, sources of food and clothing and entertainment. Humans will have to permit themselves to connect with us and share, in some small way, our feelings, our pain and our suffering. But to do this they'll first have to find and use the compassion I believe is hidden somewhere deep inside them.

J.J., Murphy and I are living the good life. We sleep in our own beds, but every morning I let Greta know that I want to join her in hers. I do this by making a few soft, high-pitched sounds. Greta says they sound like the sounds a squeaky rubber toy makes. Half asleep, she says ok, and I jump into her bed and snuggle at her side until it's time for breakfast. Sometimes for fun, Murphy and I chase each other around the property outside. He's fast, but I'm faster. Don't feel bad, I tell him. You're fast, just not as fast as a Greyhound.

"I don't feel bad, Shayna. I could never run as fast as you. You run like the wind and I love watching you."

I'm glad you feel that way, Murphy, because Greyhounds are built to run. We can run thirty-five to forty miles an hour because our heads are narrow, which permits the wind to blow over them and not interfere with our racing. We're fast because we have deep chests that hold our large lungs. Large lungs can hold lots of air, which is essential to swift racing. We're fast because we have tails that are like rudders that go in whatever direction we're going. And finally, we're fast because we're lean and strong muscled.

Yes, we were born to run and we love to run. But ever since the start of dog racing for profit, we've been bred to run and then die. Win and live. Lose and die. That's what racing is all about. But not everyone can be a winner, and eventually even winners lose. No, nobody can remain a winner forever.

Murphy may not run as fast as I, but he's a natural born acrobat. He can jump from great heights, something I won't even try to do. Indoors, I like to collect shoes and boots from the laundry room and bring them into our bedroom, where I throw them high into the air. But I don't catch them. Instead, I let them land on the floor with loud thuds. I do this over and over and over again. It's one of my favorite games.

In the summer I love to dig in the huge mountain of shavings that are in the barn. After I've dug a deep hole, I lay in it and feel cool and comfortable. I like to dig under the deck too, but Greta thinks I ought to stop because the cement blocks that support the deck might collapse. J.J. has his favorite game too. He likes to throw his red ball into the air and then catch it. He does this over and over and over again. He says he's having a ball. He's quite a guy, our J.J.

Photos by G.M.

J.J. outside enjoying the sun and springtime breezes. (April 1996)

18  My Story Ends

I think I've come to the end of my story, a story that began with a terrifying and life-threatening ordeal, but which somehow worked a miracle and turned my life around. The story of my life is the story of hundreds of thousand of Greyhound racers, but sadly theirs often don't have happy endings. Being a former racer whose brain holds a lot of memories, I can't help feeling sad at times. Depressed, too. That shouldn't surprise anyone. How can I not be depressed and sad? How can I not cry for all the racers who were and still are being retired to early graves? How can I not cry for the Disappeared Ones, for my mother and father, for my brothers and sisters? Tell me, how can I not be sad?

It's true I've been living the good life for the past six years. But I can't shake that awful depression. At least not completely. It comes and goes. I used to ask myself how I managed to survive my ordeals. And Why? Especially why. Then one day it became clear. I survived so that I might tell the story of my life to others and, by doing so, help save the lives of other racers and former racers. So that some day I might bear witness. I hope I've succeeded. I hope with all my heart I've succeeded.

We're not young anymore, and one day J.J. will stop throwing his red ball into the air, I'll stop running like the wind, and Murphy will stop performing like an acrobat. Those will be sad days, especially for Greta, because we grow old faster than she does. Sometimes I observe her looking at us, and her eyes tell me what she is thinking. She's thinking that one day she'll lose us, because no one can live forever.

And when that day comes, as one day it must, I know I'll go gently, surrounded by those I love and who love me. But I know this. I shall not be at peace, whether in this world or any other, until my brothers and sisters, by whom I mean animals everywhere regardless of species, are assured a good life and a gentle end surrounded by those they love. And that's not all. I shall not be at peace until the innocent and oppressed, whoever they are and wherever they are, regardless of species, are free and safe from harm.

Finally, I hope with all my heart that one day hunting, trapping, eating other animals, wearing them, experimenting on them and using them for so-called human sport and entertainment will be things of the past. Only then will all living beings be respected and valued; perhaps even cherished. Only then will animals of other species cease to be property, and killing them will be considered as heinous as killing humans. But first humans will have to understand and believe that to be different is not to be less. And they will have to treat us accordingly.

– Shayna
(March 1998)

PART TWO

Native American Prayer

I give you this one thought to keep –

I am with you still – I do not sleep.

I am a thousand winds that blow,

I am the diamond glints on the snow,

I am the sunlight on ripened grain,

I am the gentle autumn rain.

When you awaken in the morning's hush,

I am the swift, uplifting rush

Of quiet birds in circled flight.

I am the soft stars that shine at night.

Do not think of me as gone –

I am with you still – in each new dawn.

Epilogue I: J.J.

J.J. stopped throwing his red ball into the air sometime in April, 1998. He died a month later, on May 14. He lived fourteen years and two months. As you already know, J.J. first entered our lives when he was almost twelve and he was one of the sweetest dogs we ever knew. That's why it was so funny when he barked and growled at other dogs who approached our house. At such times his lips would curl, exposing his teeth, and he looked so ferocious that we just had to laugh. And do you remember the children's stories in which cats were said to meow, cows to moo, and dogs were supposed to bark woof-woof? Well, J.J. was the only dog we knew who actually barked woof-woof.

The end came quite suddenly, when he no longer could stand or walk, was bleeding internally and was in great pain. But, he was not alone. The veterinarian, a very special person, was present as was Greta, who kissed him and stroked him before and during his painless transition, telling him all the while how much we loved him. Now J.J. is gone. Our pain is pretty awful, but we're glad he spent the last two years and three months of his life with us. In the last few months he had become somewhat frail physically, but remained quite alert. We knew J.J. only as a dignified, elderly gentleman, and we've often wondered what he was like in his youth and prime. Quite wonderful, we're certain.

Murphy and I accepted him from the start; we felt no jealousy or resentment. Perhaps we respected him as an elder statesman even though he was only about four years older than us. As you know, J.J.'s mother and father were racers, but he never was. And as you also know, a good woman adopted him when he was two months old, and he lived the good life.

From the physical perspective, J.J. no longer is with us. But we think we believe that somewhere in some beautiful place we cannot see, J.J. once again is healthy, strong, running, woof-woofing and having a glorious time. We'll never forget him. We'll love and remember him always, as will everyone who came to know and love him after reading his thoughts and comments in my story.

– Shayna
(July 22, 1998)

Photo by G.M.

J.J., our elder statesman, two months before he died at fourteen years and two months old. (March 1998)

Death is life's twin, yet it turns joy
into sorrow and love into tears.

– from a Hebrew Prayer

Epilogue II: Shayna

Shayna stopped running like the wind on September 17, 1998. The week before, she had developed a slight limp. I brought her to the veterinary hospital and remember telling the veterinarian, "God, I hope she doesn't have bone cancer," and she replied that an x-ray would be necessary to rule it out. She left the examination room with Shayna and when they returned, the veterinarian was crying. Shayna did indeed have bone cancer.

I don't know how we made the trip home. But we did. The three of us – Shayna, Murphy and I – somehow managed to make the trip home. Three weeks later, during the early morning hours of October 10th, Shayna was in extreme pain in spite of the pain medication I gave her. She was screaming. At 7:30 that morning I phoned one of the veterinarians at home. He heard her cries and was at my house within the hour. A few minutes later my beloved Shayna, my treasured companion, was at peace; but not I. I was shattered. Why were her last hours so painful? And how would I go on without her?

Shayna is the former racer who inspired and is responsible for the legislation to end dog racing in Massachusetts. She told you that I named her Shayna because it means pretty in Yiddish. Yes, she was quite a beauty. In fact, she resembled the mother she so lovingly described. Like her mother, Shayna was brindle and white. She told you that her mother's eyes were exquisite, so exquisite they touched the soul of a four-month-old puppy. Well, Shayna's eyes were exquisite too, so exquisite they too touched the soul and were an expression of a higher spirit. It's clear to me now that she was the incarnation of a highly evolved spirit.

But Shayna was more than beautiful. She was elegant, yet warm and loving; shy, yet assertive; and she was a some-time clown. She loved to talk too, and was especially vocal during the last three weeks of her life. I'd tell her she was smarter than I because she understood my language, but I didn't quite understand hers. I tried to make a deal with a higher power; I offered a few years of my life in exchange for a few extra years for her. But my offer was refused. Now we're learning to live without her and it's such a difficult struggle...

Animals of other species ask so little of us. Most humans, on the other hand, demand so much. We talk to our animal friends and they pretty much understand us. But when they talk to us, we understand them just a little or not at all. Humans are an arrogant species. As Shayna said, the vast majority of humans mistakenly believe that other-specied animals are less than humans and treat them as such.

Humans have the power to inflict incredible pain and suffering on animals of other species and when they do, they're often acting within the framework of the law. But as world events such as the Holocaust have demonstrated, making heinous crimes legal doesn't make them less heinous.

Shayna told you that other-specied animals want to live in peace with us, but this won't happen until we find and use the compassion and love she believed are hidden somewhere deep inside us. She believed that only then would we evolve into higher spirits who wouldn't want or need to exercise control over the lives of other living creatures. She knew that gentleness and kindness go hand-in-hand with true strength, and that arrogance and brutality are symptoms of frail and weak spirits.

Shayna was a master teacher, so whenever I hear a dog bark, or a cat meow, or a cow moo, or a horse neigh, I don't hear noises. I hear sounds that are the sounds of language; unfortunately it's language I don't understand. Some persons do, and they communicate with the animals. Perhaps one day I'll learn...

Shayna is an unforgettable being and she'll live on in the legislation that was and is being filed to end dog racing in Massachusetts.

(Recently a third bill was filed.) Shayna was a magical creature while here on earth. Is she working some of her magic now that she's in heaven? Is J.J. helping her? Are Jack (a friend's beloved Greyhound who made his transition in November) and other former racers helping her? It's not impossible...

As for me, and Murphy too, it's been a struggle to go on without her. Recently another former racer joined our family. Some expected us to wait until our pain subsided. But we don't know when that will be – if ever. And we believe Shayna and J.J. would agree that saving lives is our first priority. But the pain persists. It persists even though we believe she continues to run like the wind with some of her former racing buddies and with J.J. Yes, I think we believe that somewhere, in some beautiful and faraway place that's not visible to human eyes, our cherished friends still live.

– *Greta & Murphy*
Shayna's 11th Birthday
(January 1999)

Photos by G.M.

Shayna during the last three weeks of her life. (Sept./Oct. 1998)

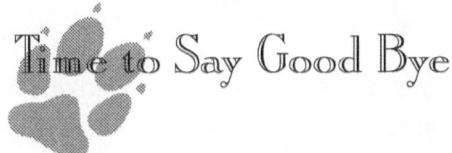 Time to Say Good Bye

Murphy is between ten-and-a-half and eleven years of age. His hair, once a deep golden blonde, has grown lighter (as has mine), his hearing isn't quite as sharp as it once was (neither is mine), and he's not quite the acrobat he once was (and I never was). I don't want to lose him too and, to paraphrase Shayna, I hope with all my heart that he stays with me for a long, long time before he leaves to join her and J.J. Murphy has been through a lot. As have I. He lost two dear friends in the short span of five months. As did I. It's not easy losing the ones you love. Everyone knows that.

In November, another former racer became a part of our family, and how naïve she was! She knew nothing about love or being part of a family. Racing had been her entire life. She started training at 6 months of age, and at eighteen months she started racing. When not racing she was confined to an undersized crate and consequently, both her hindquarters are rubbed bare.

It's not surprising that she was confused when she first arrived at her new home. To get into the house she had to climb a flight of stairs, which she somehow managed to do. Once inside, she bumped into sliding glass doors, so I pasted adhesive strips on them. Mirrors fascinated her and she'd stare at her reflection many times during the course of one day. Everything was a brand new experience!

I didn't like her racing name so I named her Diana, after the goddess who is always shown with a Greyhound at her side. It was only after she became accustomed to her name that I learned that Diana is the goddess of hunting. Hmmm... Diana is black with a white chest, four white feet and a touch of white on the tip of her tail. She's quite adorable, she'll be four sometime this month, and she last raced at a dog track in Connecticut. She was retired when she was three-and-a-half.

This affectionate and fun-loving Greyhound is inquisitive, too inquisitive for her own good. She gets into everything, and that can be dangerous. Bureau drawers must be securely closed at all times and tabletops cleared of anything of value or that might harm her. She has chewed a checkbook, eyeglass cases with and without the eyeglasses in them, and has removed a computer game and cables from a carton and chewed them. She'll chew just about anything she can get her paws and mouth on. Murphy looks at her with bewilderment. He even told an animal communicator acquaintance, "I don't want to say Diana is stupid. It's just that she's so unaware." Murphy, you're so perceptive. She is definitely unaware, but certainly not stupid.

Diana is having fun being a puppy for the first time in her four years of life, but this kind of fun puts her at risk and me in a panic. So I started confining her to a huge metal crate whenever I left the house. She likes the crate when the door is open and she can go in and out at her own free will, but not when I shut the crate door. So now, whenever I leave the house, I restrict her to a few rooms that are dog safe.

This adorable little girl loves to collect things. She likes to bring shoes and boots from the laundry room into the bedroom, as Shayna did. But Diana doesn't throw them up in the air as Shayna did. She places some of them on my bed, some in her bed, some in the crate and she leaves some of them on the floor. She does the same with hats and gloves, and it doesn't matter if they belong to me or to guests. I suppose you could call her a collector.

Diana is adjusting well to family life and she's helping us heal. Murphy and I love her dearly. But we miss gentle J.J. and lovely Shayna. We miss our two cherished friends and we'll remember and love them always. Their transition to a better and more beautiful place broke our hearts. But we're trying to find some comfort in the belief that life transcends the physical plane and they moved from this life into another. And we're trying to find some comfort in the belief that

J.J. and Shayna had completed their journey on earth, and it was time for them to say goodbye.

– Murphy & Greta
Diana's 4th Birthday
(March 1999)

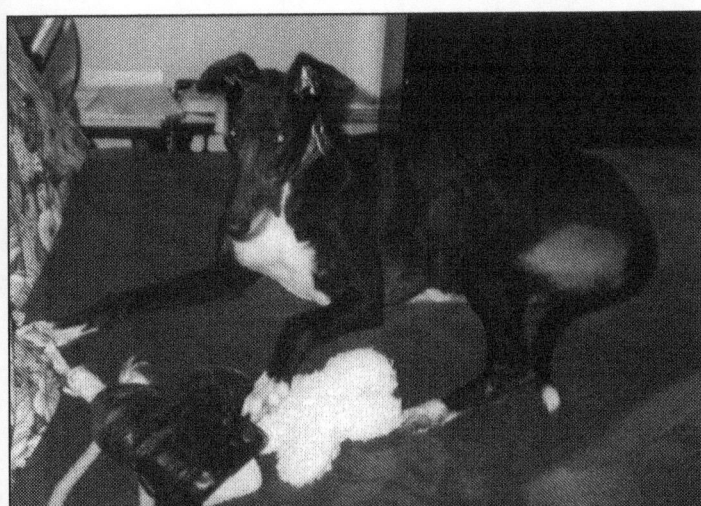

At Left: Diana inside with her toy and one of Greta's shoes. Notice the bald area on her hind quarter. (Nov. 1998)

Below: Diana outside. (April 2000)

Photos by G.M.

Go rejoice, and remember me;
you know how we have loved you here...

– from Sappho
(as translated by Anne Burnett)

Epilogue III: Murphy

Murphy no longer is with us. He's with J.J. and Shayna, and he too left suddenly and with almost no warning. In the previous chapter I wrote that I hoped Murphy would stay with me for a long, long time before he left to join J.J. and Shayna. But he didn't, and it's not easy to keep saying goodbye.

It started quite subtly on the morning of Monday, January 10th, when it was raining furiously and Murphy exhibited signs of arthritis for the very first time. Arthritis isn't a life-threatening disease, at least I don't believe it is. Yet I felt unreasonably anxious and cancelled an appointment with a friend so that I might stay at home with him. Buffered aspirin relieved the symptoms for just a few days, and then an examination and x-rays confirmed that he did indeed have arthritis. But while examining Murphy, the veterinarian discovered a mass in his mouth, which he was certain was malignant. According to the biopsy report that was received on January 19th, it was malignant melanoma. I wasn't just horrified (malignant melanoma had killed my father), I was stunned because just a few months earlier one of Murphy's canine teeth had to be removed after an accidental kick in the face by a horse. At that time his mouth had appeared perfectly healthy.

After chest x-rays and blood tests revealed nothing abnormal, surgery was scheduled for Monday, January 24th. But this was not to be because on the morning of January 21st, Murphy started dragging one hind leg. An hour later his other hind leg was affected and he could neither stand nor walk. He had lost the use of both legs. An employee at the veterinary clinic drove to my house and placed Murphy in my car so that I could drive him to the hospital. There it was determined that he probably had suffered a severe extrusion of a spinal disk. Murphy was a paraplegic. Surgery to remove the melanoma was cancelled.

I had rescued Murphy from certain death in a shelter on Long Island, NY. Actually it wasn't a shelter. A group of women were rescuing dogs from a municipal shelter as well as from the streets. They would board them in a private facility until they found homes for them. Murphy had lived on the streets for some time before being brought to a municipal shelter. Shortly before he was to be put to death, he was rescued by one of the women and placed in the private facility. After living in the facility for seven months he hadn't been adopted. The women were running out of money to pay for his board, and Murphy was running out of time.

One of the women placed an ad in a local newspaper that read, "Teddy bear of a dog desperately needs a home. Please help!" I phoned the woman, told her I wanted to adopt the dog who was advertised in the newspaper, and picked him up on the way home from work later that day. That's how Murphy and I entered each other's lives. At first, because I was accustomed to small dogs, Murphy (who weighed about sixty pounds) looked like a giant to me.

I always had the feeling that a bit of the wild lived in Murphy. Not only did he look like a cross between a coyote and a wolf (sometimes I called him my coyote-wolf boy), he craved freedom like the wild ones do. He demonstrated this need to be free whenever I walked him on a leash. At such times he'd jump so high I thought he was trying to reach the sky. He was an acrobat, too, often jumping from the deck to the ground instead of using the stairs. Could this have caused the severe injury to his spinal disk? Or had the melanoma metastasized? I don't know. I do know Murphy was happiest when running around the property wearing his battery collar and protected by the invisible fencing that surrounded him. It was quite a sight to watch him and Shayna run and run and run. As he said, he didn't mind one bit that Shayna ran faster than he.

My coyote-wolf boy had quite a personality. Upon returning home from the supermarket I would place my groceries and fruits and vegetables on the kitchen counter and he would help me put the fruits and vegetables away in his own special way. He'd stand on his two hind legs and, using one of his front legs, he'd sweep them onto the floor and munch away until I observed him and retrieved the remains of a week's supply of salad and fruit. Some years ago he swept a cantaloupe off the counter top and ate every bit of it – skin, seeds and sweet fruit. I was concerned and phoned the veterinarian, who said he'd probably not suffer any ill affects. And he didn't.

Murphy loved broccoli, carrots, celery cabbage and bok choy, and if he didn't get them via the kitchen counter, he'd take them out of the refrigerator whenever I opened the refrigerator door. And then there were the bananas. He'd sweep them onto the floor too, and just three weeks ago he tore open their plastic wrapping, peeled off the skins and ate two of them before I realized what was happening. He was very special, my Murphy, and I'm going to miss him desperately once the protective veil of numbness leaves me and his passing becomes devastating reality.

I brought him home because I wanted him to die at home. My friend, Scott, carried him from my car into the house. During his last few days of life I sang to him, hugged him, kissed him and read him a story I'd written years ago called, "Murphy and Shayna: The story of Two Good Friends." I talked to him too, and told him that a nice man would be coming who'd send him on a journey that would bring him to a beautiful place where J.J. and Shayna lived. I fed him some of his favorite treats, including veggie patties, flavored yogurt, vegetarian strips that taste like bacon, and apple-raisin vegan dog biscuits.

During Shayna's last three weeks of life Murphy knew something was terribly wrong and he nuzzled, sniffed and kissed her often. Now Diana knew something was terribly wrong and she did the same to Murphy. Indeed, for the two days and nights before he died she lay at his side, something she'd never done before. And during this time she developed an intestinal ailment, which continues as of this writing, and which the veterinarian believes is the result of severe anxiety and stress. Persons who say other-specied animals don't feel sadness, empathy and compassion for others are simply fools.

On the afternoon of January 23rd, Murphy was euthanized in the bedroom we had shared together for so many years. I believe he was ready to go. And I was ready to let him go. It was time for him to leave his body which had always been so healthy, strong and beautiful, but which now had become a merciless trap in a matter of days. He was surrounded by persons who loved him, and during his painless transition, Diana and I, and our friends Joanne and Hillary, kissed him and hugged him, stroked him gently and told him how much we loved him.

Goodbye my handsome Murphy, my magnificent coyote-wolf boy. Good-bye my beloved friend. You completed your journey here on earth. Now go rejoice with J.J. and Shayna in that far away, beautiful place that's invisible to mortal eyes. And please remember us. Remember, all three of you, how we have loved you here.

– Diana & Greta
(January 26, 2000)

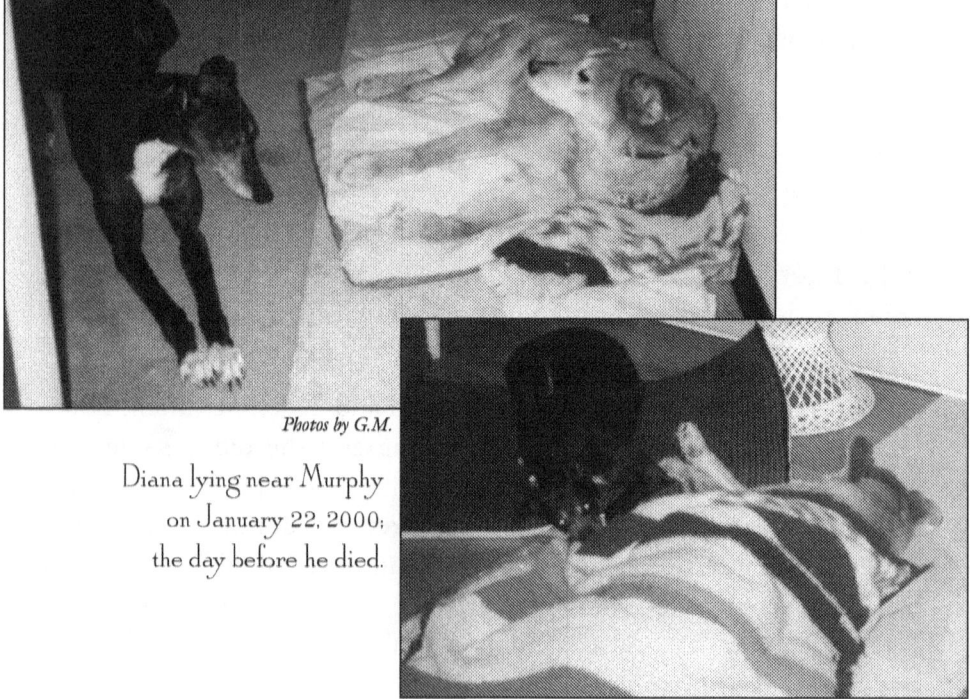

Photos by G.M.

Diana lying near Murphy
on January 22, 2000;
the day before he died.

Loved ones die and life goes on.

Dealer's Story

I just turned five in March 2000. I raced at Raynham/Taunton Greyhound Park. I must have been good because I was retired only about four months ago. I raced for one of the kennels there, but just didn't have it in me anymore. They took me to Boyd's "retirement" farm in Taunton, MA. People came from a few adoption groups to get dogs, but none of them wanted me because I'm black. I also didn't show as much affection as the other dogs. So after about three months, Terry from the retirement farm mentioned me to Robin (Norton). She knows that all she has to do is mention a greyhound's name and – if she attaches even the tiniest hint of a sad story to it – Robin becomes obsessed and she must save that dog.

So that's all she said: "No one wants him, he's black." And Robin said, "I do. I'll take him." I heard her say that. I really did. She didn't even have to take me out of my cage to make the decision. But when she did, she said, "He's beautiful. Why would no one want him?" Hearing these words made me feel so good. Then she picked out this silly, crazy, brindle girl named Pet. And off we went to Greysland. On the way home, Robin changed Pet's name to Penny. She asked, "Who would name their beautiful greyhound 'Pet'?"

So, this is my reward for being a "greyt" racer? It certainly was worth the wait. Robin bathed me and it felt so good to be clean. The water ran off me black into her tub. Sleeping on shredded newspaper definitely has its disadvantages. Imagine if I were a white greyhound! I got a manicure, my ears were cleaned, and I got the softest bed to sleep on. It was Heaven. The chow was good, too. (Even though Robin slipped some worming medicine in it – she thinks I don't know.) Most of all, I liked the ear scratches and all the attention. Oh, I liked the stuffed animals and tennis balls, too. I get kind of possessive about them, though. That's because I never had so many good things and now I just don't want to lose them. Henry is worse than me when it comes to that; so there.

I went to see Dr. Jill the next day. She gave me my vaccines and did a heartworm test. I visited her a week later and got neutered. It was no big deal (no pun intended). I went for lots of walks with Robin or Jini or Sherry. (I do pretty well on a leash, but I'd like to get my paws on one of those squirrels.) Sherry loves me a lot. She said she wanted to take me home so many times, but her husband said, "We aren't having three dogs!"

Sherry took me to her house on Thursday night and gave me a bath so I'd look real special for Diana and Greta. She also gave me a bag of treats (she makes them at home), and I think I'll share them with Diana.

I'm kind of nervous to make that trip tomorrow. I know that Greta and Diana will love me a lot, but I get nervous on long trips. Just don't want to ever be sent back to the track. Life is good now, and it's about to get better.

UPDATE: I'm in my new home now and Greta changed my name to Danny Boy, the name of one of her favorite songs. I can feel that she and Diana love me, and I know that I'm going to love them back. I like retirement!

Photo by G.M.

> *– Danny Boy,*
> *formerly known as Dealer*
> (April 2000)
>
>
> *"Dealer's Story" was written*
> *by Robin Norton, founder of*
> *Greysland Greyhound Adoption*
> *in Hopkinton, MA.*

Danny Boy with a stuffed animal. (April 2000)

Photos by G.M.

Danny Boy (above) and Danny Boy
with Diana (below). (April 2000)

Do not stand at my grave and weep.
I am not there. I do not sleep.

– Anonymous

We do not stand at your graves and weep.
We know you're not there. We know you don't sleep.

– Diana, Danny Boy & Greta
(April 2000)

Phots by G.M.

THOUGHTFUL MOMENTS

Diana (above) and
Danny Boy (below).

Terri

On November 5, 1998, a little brindle girl named Terri came into our lives. She was the teeniest greyhound with the biggest ears I ever met! It wasn't our plan to adopt another greyhound because we already had six. Jack, one of our first greyhounds, was still with us at the time, and we had just gotten Cozy a year before. I found a home for Terri with a wonderful family in Rhode Island.

Fate had it that I had somehow gotten myself a greyhound puppy! What the heck was I thinking? Well, it turns out that Terri wasn't really happy in her new home and I wasn't really happy having a puppy, so I made a deal with Dixie. "I'll take Terri but you have to take the puppy." She was thrilled and so was I. Terri was the most perfect greyhound ever. She had the best nature and got along with everyone: kids, cats, other dogs, you name it. She became my little ambassador at Meet and Greets. She was so perfect that everyone who met her wanted a Terri, too. No way was I giving her up again. She became my little singing senorita. Every morning she would serenade me (5 to 6 am was not my favorite time, but oh well).

Then, in November of 2000, she stopped singing. It took months to figure out why. She finally was diagnosed with auto-immune meningitis (aka GME). For a while we were able to keep her well and comfortable, but in the last few months the nasty disease, and the medication she was on to fight it, had taken a toll on her. With her suppressed immune system she was unable to fight off even the simplest of infections.

Today (February 20, 2002) we made the heartwrenching decision to let her go. It seems so unfair. She was so young, only six-and-a-half. She was my baby, the youngest of my five. Terri will live forever in my heart, along with Jack and Josie. I know she is better now and that she accepted her death. Dogs just do. She told me that.

Now if only I could.

– Robin Norton
Founder of Greysland
Greyhounds Adoption, Inc.,
in Hopkinton, MA.

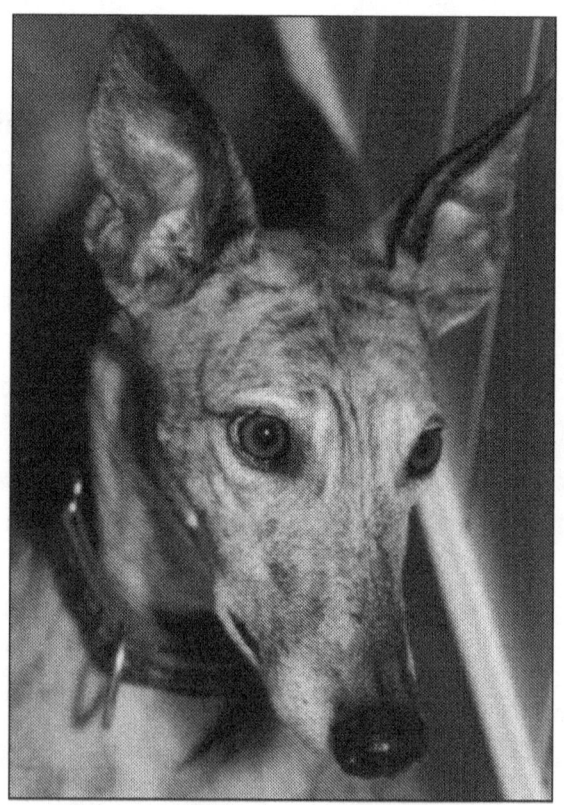

Photo by Robin Norton.

Terri: Aug. 4, 1995 to Feb. 20, 2002.

We do not stand at your grave and weep.
We know you're not there.
We know you don't sleep.

– Robin, Jack, Justin, Michael and
greyhounds Sara, Jasmine, Cozy and Vikki
(February 2002)

PART THREE

Additional Information –

As it Relates to Certain Previous Chapters (1, 2, 7, 9, 10, 11, 12, 13, 14, 16) and Epilogues (2, 3)

Endnotes

"No one can shut his eyes and pretend that
the evil which is invisible to him doesn't exist."

– Albert Schweitzer

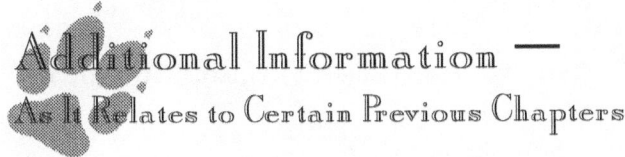

Additional Information —
As It Relates to Certain Previous Chapters

List of Abbreviations

MaCADR – Massachusetts Citizens Against Dog Racing

GNN – Greyhound Network News

GPL – Greyhound Protection League

PCRM – Physicians Committee for Responsible Medicine

IDA – In Defense of Animals

USDA – United States Department of Agriculture

NIH – National Institutes of Health

TFC – The Coulston Foundation

NGA – National Greyhound Association

CSU – Colorado State University

AVAR – Association of Veterinarians for Animal Rights

IPPL – International Primate Protection League

Chapter 1. Abandoned

Shayna was discovered in a Massachusetts cemetery in winter. She was wearing her racing muzzle.

Only Shayna knows how she got there.

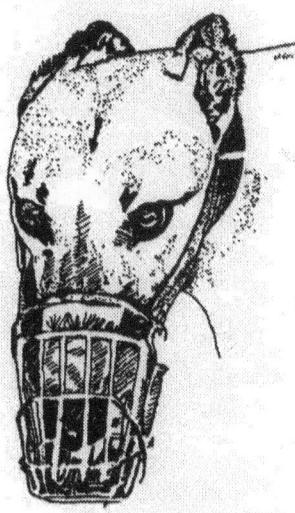
Poster courtesy of the Greyhound Protection League.

Chapter 2. The Beginning
(puppy murder)

Susan Netboy, Greyhound Protection League founder, wrote the following which relates to Chapter 2.

> Take one look into the eyes of a greyhound –
> you will see all the innocent souls who have
> died before their time … and at that moment
> you will join the millions of others
> who will never, never forget.

Ironically, the first step in the struggle for survival for a racing greyhound is to overcome the perils of the dog farm and "graduate" to a cage at a racetrack. The death defying attempts to prove himself begin at birth with the struggle to make his tiny body look like a winner when first confronted with the scent of a human hand reaching into the whelping box. That challenge will have to be met over and over again throughout his career. None, in fact, are immune from the harsh reality of culling: even "spent winners" are likely to be revisited by the memory of that scent during the last moments of their young lives. Twenty percent of all greyhound puppies "disappear" prior to being registered for racing at eighteen months of age. Some pups are destroyed at birth, some die from preventable diseases such as distemper and parvo, others die from injuries incurred during the training process; but the vast majority are killed because they fail to show promise as money makers at the track. Tragically, in the 1990s alone, nearly 90,000 puppies "disappeared" from the farms before they ever had a racing career.

Once a greyhound has entered the racing system, the odds for survival get even worse. Each time a race dog explodes out of the starting box he or she is at risk of suffering a career or life-ending injury. However, it is the failure to make money that is the most menacing threat to a race dog and most will succumb to that risk before the age of three. Longevity is a rare commodity in the world of dog racing; the effects of marginal care, sub-standard diet and minor injuries will eventually catch up with even the most successful racer. Less than 8% of the 40,000 race dogs incarcerated at North American tracks are still racing at five years of age.

During its seventy-five-year history in America, dog racing has been responsible for the immense suffering and death of more than a million greyhounds. The industry's enforcement of the "code of silence" served it well until the early 1990s, when main stream media stories referencing "body counts" of up to 50,000 greyhounds a year started seeping into living rooms across America and cruel methods of killing, including starvation, electrocution and shooting became widely publicized. The industry's callous disregard for the very entity which lined its pockets with billions of dollars, was met with unprecedented outrage and condemnation by both the animal welfare community and the American public. After experiencing a meteoric rise in the world of exploiting and killing animals for profit, greyhound racing was faced with a public relations debacle. Fortunately, out of the rubble of one relentless exposé after another, the greyhound adoption movement was born. Where as the maxim "Win or Die" used to apply to nearly every race dog hauled into a track compound, the odds for survival have increased in recent years. Through the valiant efforts of greyhound rescue groups, tens of thousands of gentle greyhounds have survived racing and made the transition from racing commodity to treasured family companion. However, as we enter the 21st century, the kill trucks are far from idle; for in spite of nationwide rescue efforts, thousands upon thousands of greyhounds continue to be killed year after year.

Although the greyhound racing industry has itself suffered a near death experience in recent years with revenues dropping as much as 70%, it continues to be resuscitated with bailouts and tax breaks meted out by track friendly legislators whose interest in campaign contributions supercedes the ethics of the new millennium. While dog track tycoons and their high-paid lobbyists haunt the halls of state capitals currying favor with aging legislators, the other arm of the industry's survivalist team, the public relations specialists, prepare their client for the latest version of the public relations make-over – the new face of dog racing: the one that claims that greyhound welfare and adoption are its greatest concern, the one that states that greyhounds love to be muzzled and caged, the one that says that greyhounds are treated better than most people treat their children. Yes, we've all heard it; and, sadly, some believe it. But fortunately, the majority of people are not deceived by this futile attempt to rewrite history. They know that nowadays the bodies are as well hidden as the industry's agenda; and that the killing fields, mass burial pits and incinerators are merely deeper and more remote. They understand the manipulation of rescue groups. And they recognize the industry's newfound concern for the greyhounds as nothing more than a masquerade – a public relations ploy designed to erase its unconscionably brutal history from public consciousness, so that the greyhound racing industry will once again be positioned to pursue its long-term goal of entrenchment and expansion into all fifty states.

"Those who can't remember the past are doomed to relive it."

– *George Santayna*
(1863-1952)

Figures cited are based on an analysis of industry breeding numbers and pari-mutuel gaming resources.

– *Susan Netboy*

The Greyhound Protection League (GPL) was founded by Susan Netboy in 1991. It is a national organization that rescues racers and exposes Greyhound cruelty and abuse nation and worldwide. "The GPL," Susan writes, "is dedicated to the hundreds and thousands of greyhounds who have been rewarded for service to the industry with death in the prime of life." The GPL may be contacted at: Greyhound Protection League, P.O. Box 669, Penn Valley CA 95946; (800) 446-8637.

"Greyhounds are bred to make money and when they slow down and lose a few races, they aren't considered worthy of food and minimal care. They worked hard for a living and earned their keep. But they must die as cheaply as possible. This holocaust of greyhounds must stop.

There surely is a special place in hell waiting for those who inflict such pain and suffering upon fine, noble and gentle dogs. Sooner or later this greedy industry will self-destruct. I intend to help in that endeavor."

– Erika Hartmen
San Antonio, Texas (1994)

Epitaph for a Greyhound

She was the 8th dog in the 12th race on a cold and rainy Saturday night at Tuscon Greyhound Park. Loaded into the starting box, wearing a racing silk of yellow and black, the colors for the 8th and outside position, four-year-old Figs Greta, favored to win, was ready to run her last $\frac{5}{16}$-mile race on a muddy track.

The starter gave the signal, the gates opened and the race began. Early into the first turn she was bumped hard and fell. Regaining her footing, disoriented despite her years of experience, she began to run in the opposite direction. The sideline handlers ran to intercept her but she turned again, this time heading for the infield.

In one last desperate leap she tried to clear the electrified rail. In all probability, the voltage killed her instantly so she never felt the returning mechanical lure strike her lifeless body, exploding her chest from the impact.

As the lead-outs finally reached her, the track lights went out ... no need for patrons to see the blood-covered handlers lifting her once-beautiful white and black body from the rail that killed her, or the bloodied and mangled forever-ahead mechanical rabbit that mutilated her.

For Figs Greta, the last race was over.

Figs Greta
April 11, 1988 – December 5, 1992

"Epitaph for a Greyhound," written by Joan Eidenger and reprinted with her permission, appeared in the Spring 1993 edition of the Greyhound Network News (GNN). Ms. Eidenger also wrote, "This issue is dedicated to Figs Greta and the countless number of unknown greyhounds whose necks and legs have been broken or who have been electrocuted on racetracks across America."

The GNN was founded as a result of the Chandler Heights Massacre. In January 1992, the decomposing bodies of 143 former racers were discovered in an abandoned apple orchard not far from Phoenix, AZ.

Ears with their identifying tattoos had been cut off so that the person or persons responsible for this heinous crime could not be traced. But some ears were found and traced to a particular kennel operator. He was charged with criminal littering, a felony, fined $25,000 and his license was revoked. He was ordered to perform community service and he was excluded from the national organization.

The GNN is a publication devoted to Greyhound racers and former racers nation and worldwide. It is a must for persons who wish to keep informed about the plight of these gentle dogs and the status of dog racing state, nation and worldwide. Its publisher is Joan Eidenger and it depends upon donations from its readers to cover the costs of publication. To subscribe, contact the GNN at:Greyhound Network News, P.O. Box 44272, Phoenix AZ 85064.

Chapter 7. There's No Such Thing as a Slow Greyhound — No One Can Remain a Winner Forever (accidents and abuse)

Collisions, falls and other racetrack injuries are not isolated incidents. Some require immediate euthanasia and, when not forthcoming, racers die slowly and in great pain. The following are just a few examples. Untold numbers of such accidents go unreported.

In late June, 2000, a petite fifty-five-pound racer was killed while racing at Raynham/Taunton Greyhound Park in Taunton, MA. Her name was Midget, she was twenty-one months old, and she was racing in her maiden (introductory) race. As she approached her first turn, she got caught between several other racers, lost her footing, fell, and was trampled by the other dogs. She sustained a broken neck and died instantly. (*Source:* GPL Facts Sheet, October 2000.) It's not unusual for large and small racers of the same grade to compete in the same races.

In February 2000, the Animal Rescue League of Boston, MA, was seeking a criminal complaint against the *owner* of ten Greyhounds. Suffering from long-term and severe malnutrition and injuries, the dogs were being housed in a kennel in Taunton, MA, near the Raynham/Taunton dog track. One of the officers assigned to the case said it was one of the worst cases of neglect he'd seen in twelve years as an investigator. The *owner*, Kevin Holloway, was charged with six counts of cruelty.

These former racers, who were being used for breeding purposes, were in horrendous condition. A four-year-old named Rosie had a mauled foot, a broken leg and infected, open wounds. Red, a nine-year-old male, had a long gash on his face and a huge lump on his back, possibly a hernia.

According to the veterinarian who treated them, both were infested with fleas and open, draining wounds, and Rosie was extremely emaciated. A photo of another nine-year-old male, Henry, shows a dog in skeletal condition. His spleen had to be removed. Also included were a ten-year-old female who recently had been bred, and some puppies under a year old. All were expected to recover. (*Source: Boston Globe, 2-9-2000, and the Metrowest Daily News, 2-7-2000.*)

On June 21, 2000, at the Birmingham, AL, dog track, a racer named Randad was electrocuted when he climbed onto the lure rail, which is electrically similar to a subway's hot rail. According to witnesses, Randad shrieked for several seconds until he was struck and killed by the mechanical lure which the dogs chase and which rotates around the track. (*Source: GNN and Birmingham News, Benjamin Niolet, 6-29-2000.*)

On March 3, 2000, Dr. Harry Roland, a dentist in private practice in Texas, was arrested and charged with animal cruelty after he failed to obtain veterinary treatment for an injured racer. On Jan. 6, 2000, Corky's Scanner, two-and-a-half, who had been leased to Roland, broke his leg while racing at the Corpus Christie dog track in Texas. He was returned to Roland's breeding and training farm in Hutto, which is near Austin, where he received no medical treatment.

When Corky's *owner* learned that he had been injured, she tried to have him returned to her. When that failed she filed a complaint against Roland with the National Greyhound Association, the national organization in the U.S. Its one full-time inspector located Corky, but the kennel manager wouldn't allow him to take the dog.

Because he needed immediate medical treatment, Corky's *owner* contacted the Houston chapter of Greyhound Pets of America, an adoption group. Two GPA persons then drove to Hutto and contacted the sheriff's office for help in retrieving Corky. It was reported that while fifty feet away from the kennel building, the officer and two women were overwhelmed by the stench of urine that came from it. Once inside the building, they found Corky and twenty-four other Greyhounds lying in small (2′ by 4′) wooden cages with no bedding of any kind. Food and water bowls were nowhere to be seen and all of the dogs were muzzled. One dog appeared to be injured and the kennel manager said he had a "hurt back."

Corky's broken leg was swollen and infected. The bandage that had been wrapped around his leg by the track veterinarian hadn't been changed in forty-six days! Under questioning, Dr. Roland said, "I choose not to pay for it (surgery) and I choose to let the dog, the leg heal on its own if it can... The ones ... I just want to use as broods, I usually don't have them set, because of the expense. That's the bottom line." Corky's body was covered with ulcerated sores, he suffered from a staff infection throughout his body and he was unable to walk. He was carried to a waiting vehicle and transported to Houston for medical treatment.

Three days later, on 2-24-2000, two sheriff's deputies returned to the farm and found Greyhounds housed in three hauling trailers and in the kennel building. Those housed in the latter were described as quite lethargic. In addition, three injured rabbits, who probably were used for training purposes, were found in a cage. According to the kennel manager, between 160 and 175 Greyhounds were housed on the farm. On March 1, sheriff's deputies accompanied by a veterinarian returned to Roland's farm with a court-ordered search and seizure warrant and executed the warrant by searching the premises. When they couldn't find the approximately sixty sick and injured dogs they had come for, it became clear that they had been removed. The kennel manager said they "were taken to the track to race." When asked about the dog with the bad back, he said he too had been "taken to the races."

The GPA director and some volunteers who had planned on returning to Houston with the sick and injured dogs, left without them. They had been removed sometime before March 1. The Greyhound Protection League posted a $2,000 reward for information leading to the safe recovery of the dogs, but it's believed they were killed. During a search of Roland's farm, sheriff's deputies discovered a feces dump containing skeletons as well as decaying bodies. A few had been killed recently, and bleeding from their noses and ears indicated they had died from a trauma to the head. Also found was a tree with a chain around it, a pool of blood and a large metal pipe with dried blood on the end.

Under questioning, the kennel man admitted he had beaten one Greyhound to death with the metal pipe (the dog with the "hurt back"), and had suffocated another. Both he and Roland were arrested and held on $5,000 bond each. Roland posted his bail and was released. He was charged with a misdemeanor. A misdemeanor! The kennel manager, who admitted to committing the murders, was jailed. The National Greyhound Association (NGA) scheduled a disciplinary hearing for April 22, 2000. (*Source:* The Greyhound Network News, Spring 2000, pp. 1 and 7.)

After Dr. Roland agreed to hire additional help, he was permitted to keep the remaining Greyhounds at his farm and the county sheriff's department was supposed to be carefully watching the farm. (*Source:* The Greyhound Review, a publication of the National Greyhound Association, April 2000, p. 3.) At the disciplinary hearing in late April, Roland was excluded from membership in the NGA and was given until July 1 to transfer any Greyhounds out of his name. (*Source:* The Greyhound Review, June 2000.)

The case was prosecuted by the Williamstown County District Attorney's Office, and on August 29, 2000, the defendant pled guilty to misdemeanor charges of animal cruelty. He was sentenced to two years probation, fined $4,000, and ordered to make a $5,000 donation to the Williamstown Humane Society. He was prohibited from owning dogs or participating in racing until after his probation ended. (*Source:* GNN, Fall 2000, pp. 1 and 7.)

On February 23, 2000, at the Naples, Florida, dog track, eye witnesses and media reported that racer Tune Me In was bumped by at least one other dog, became disoriented and ran into the pole that supports the mechanical lure (which the dogs chase). The rotating mechanical lure then sliced her shoulder blades. Tune Me In bled profusely and screamed in agony. Everyone, patrons and track personnel alike, heard her cries and several patrons complained to track officials for ignoring the dog's pain and suffering. When they received no satisfaction, an eyewitness contacted a local TV station and spoke to one of its reporters, who asked for permission to view the videotape of the race. Her request was denied, and no attempts were made to help the dog until the announcer declared the race null and void. Tune Me In suffered in agony for twenty to thirty minutes and had just about bled to death before she finally was euthanized. Track officials said the delay occurred because they had to contact her *owner* before she could be euthanized.

The Greyhound Protection League filed a cruelty complaint with the Florida Division of Parimutuel Wagering, and on March 17th, that agency completed its investigation. It ruled that track officials had acted properly, and there was no violation of Florida's anti-cruelty laws or parimutuel racing rules. (*Source:* GNN, Spring 2000.)

Sometime in the year 2000, many racers perished in a West Virginia kennel when its central air conditioning unit failed. The National Greyhound Association (NGA) then suggested – it probably doesn't have the authority to mandate – that all kennel *owners* who use central air conditioning units install alarm systems that would alert them in the event of a failure. (*Source:* The Greyhound Review, publication of the NGA, December 2000, p. 127.)

In late summer 1999, Arizona Greyhound Rescue filed a complaint with the Arizona Racing Commission against trainer/*owner* Johnny Rippetoe after learning that upon his demand in June, seventeen racers had been put to death at Pima County Animal Control. It was charged that he had violated the state racing code, which required that every effort be made to adopt out Greyhounds who aren't used for racing or breeding purposes.

The dogs had been racing at Tuscon Greyhound Park and all were healthy and adoptable. Sixteen were between two and four years old, and one was nine. Mr. Rippetoe said adoption groups didn't take them fast enough, which left him with the burden of feeding dogs who weren't bringing in any money. It was easier to put them to death, he said, and when he did, he felt "real bad." He also said, "if you're going to be in this business, you have to be mean." Soon thereafter, Pima Animal Control changed its policy of putting racers to death upon demand. Consequently, when Mr. Rippetoe brought in eight more racers to be destroyed in August, Pima Animal Control contacted both Arizona Greyhound Rescue as well as a track-approved group whose holding pen is reported to be located in the same compound as Mr. Rippetoe's racing kennel. The eight retired racers were placed in adoptive homes.

Mr. Rippetoe described Tuscon Greyhound Park as an end-of-the-line track, where the oldest and slowest racers go, which is why, he said, so many dogs end their racing careers there. (*Source:* GNN, Fall 1999.)

NOTE: *Mr. Rippetoe said you have to be mean to be in this business. Perhaps this is why trainers with a conscience have left and are leaving the dog racing business.*

A woman turned her racer into a shelter in Florida and told shelter staff that the dog's strange-looking nose was the result of a birth defect. But x-rays indicated that the racer had been struck so hard on the side of her face that both her muzzle and lower jaw had been broken. Also shown in the x-rays was a bullet lodged in her tongue. She was rescued by Michigan Retired Greyhounds as Pets and eventually was adopted. (*Source:* GNN, Winter 1998/1999.)

When the Greenetrack dog track, a seasonal track in Eutaw, AL, abruptly ended its racing season on Sept. 6, 1998, 350 racers were at risk. Adoption groups rescued 212, but the remainder were sent to three end-of-the-line tracks in Florida; one closed just weeks after some of the dogs arrived. Their fate remains unknown. A number of adoption and other groups joined forces to rescue the 212 at a cost of almost $30,000. Four racers required emergency veterinary care. One had a broken leg, which his trainer had "grotesquely" set, two had amputated tails, and one required seven surgeries due to injuries sustained in a dogfight. It was reported that The National Greyhound Association (NGA) contributed nothing to this rescue effort.

Greenetrack is known as a "killing field," and it has been reported that its kennels are dank and dark with broken-down, makeshift wood and wire crates that are very difficult to clean. The dirt in the outside runs have never been replaced with clean dirt, and when it rains the stench is unbearable, the water mixes with the urine and feces that have been there for years, and the dogs stand ankle deep in feces-urine muck. (*Source:* GNN, Winter 1998/1999.)

In January 1997, nine starved racers from the Plainfield Greyhound Park in Connecticut, were brought to a local veterinary clinic. They were covered with sores, fleas and ticks. Some were more than 20 pounds underweight; one was suffering from kidney failure, and was unconscious and near death. The veterinarian said, "They were all basically starving." (*Source:* The Hartford Courant, January 1997, and GNN, Winter 1996/1997.)

In an interview in the PitchWeekly, a Kansas City, Kansas, newspaper, a former trainer and kennel owner said, "over the fifteen years I was in the business, I probably killed about 1,500 dogs. I usually shot them in the head." (*Source:* GNN, Winter 1999/2000.)

Last Minute Alert/Update

On May 21, 2002, in Lillian, AL, law enforcement personnel discovered a grave with the bodies of between 1,000 and 3,000 Greyhounds. They had been shot in the mouth or neck. Robert Rhodes, the owner of the property, admitted murdering the dogs and said trainers from the nearby Pensacola Greyhound Track, in Florida, sent him the dogs and paid him ten dollars for each Greyhound he murdered. He said he had been doing this for decades. He was charged with three counts of animal cruelty, a felony, and could be jailed for up to ten years. (Could be, but will he be?) The county district attorney described the scene as a "Dachau for dogs." (*Source:* The New York Times, May 24, 2002, and the Tuscaloosa News, May 23, 2002.)

But Rhodes isn't the only killer. The trainers who sent him the dogs and paid him $10 for each one he murdered, and the track officials who permitted this to go on for so many decades are equally, if not more, responsible. A horrendous crime? Yes. Heartbreaking? Yes. Shocking? No! It happens all the time, but most massacres go undetected. This is the nature of dog racing and it can't be changed.

Be aware that large numbers of the murder victims raced in a variety of states before ending up in Florida.

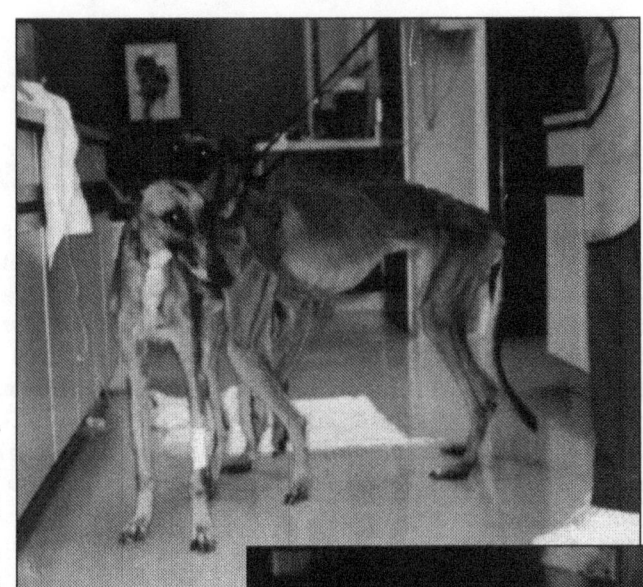

Two of ten former Greyhound racers found in a locked kennel in Phoenix, AZ. (March 1993)

Photos by Howard Bernstein (husband of GNN founder).

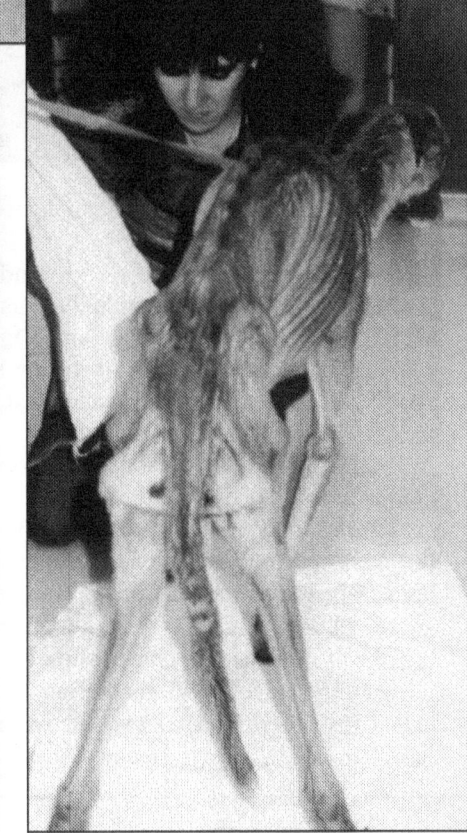

GABRIEL'S STORY:
A Happy Ending

In late February, a muzzled two-year-old male greyhound was found crawling into a shed somewhere in south central Texas. Near death from the horrendous wounds covering his swollen body, he was brought to the Austin Human Society Shelter to be euthanized.

He was placed on the table and as the veterinarian prepared to inject the sodium pentobarbital solution that would end the dog's suffering forever, the doctor looked into the eyes of the fawn-colored greyhound and saw in them a spark of life and a will to live. In  that moment the choice was made to spare the greyhound's life.

Gentle hands then began to clean and medicate the 13″ diameter wound on his back and the multiple thigh and leg wounds. The muzzle-damaged disfigured lips would have to wait. If he survived, they could be surgically repaired later.

As the days passed and his condition gradually improved, Beverly Ratzlaff of the Greyhound Protection League (Austin) attempted to find him an adoptive home. But no one wanted a badly injured and disfigured dog who would require months of nursing care and possible future surgery. Out of options, Ms. Ratzlaff called Erika Hartman, newly settled in San Antonio after moving from Vermont,

where she had spent years organizing demonstrations at Green Mountain track.

After hearing the details of the story, Erika said of course she would take him, and several days later she drove the 150 miles to Austin and brought him home. She called him Gabriel.

"I was afraid his large wounds would start bleeding, so I treated him very gingerly. I spoke to him in soft tones and told him that he must trust me, because we will be together for a long time. His soft eyes observed me and I made no quick movements, as he would jump at even the sound of a leaf breaking in the grass. He was afraid of everything and of all men. I slept with him on the floor during the first night. I wanted to make certain that he knew I was there. I touched him often and he slept well."

Under Erika's round-the-clock care, Gabriel has recovered his strength and his wounds are almost healed. On May 12 surgery was successfully done to repair his disfigured lips and he will soon be the beautiful greyhound he once was.

Abused and abandoned by the industry that bred him, spared from the needle of death by the merciful veterinarian who treated him, Gabriel has at last come home to love and human kindness.

Long life, Gabriel.

"Gabriel's Story" reprinted courtesy of GREYHOUND NETWORK NEWS, *Summer 1993.*

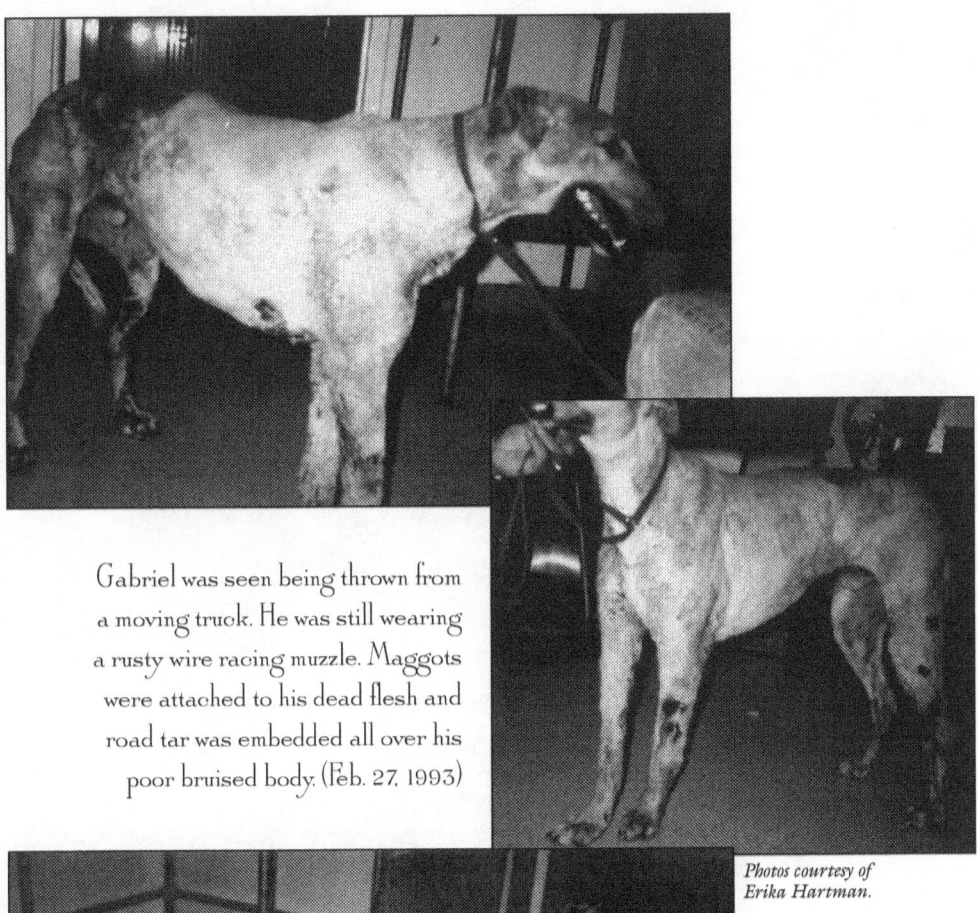

Gabriel was seen being thrown from a moving truck. He was still wearing a rusty wire racing muzzle. Maggots were attached to his dead flesh and road tar was embedded all over his poor bruised body. (Feb. 27, 1993)

Photos courtesy of Erika Hartman.

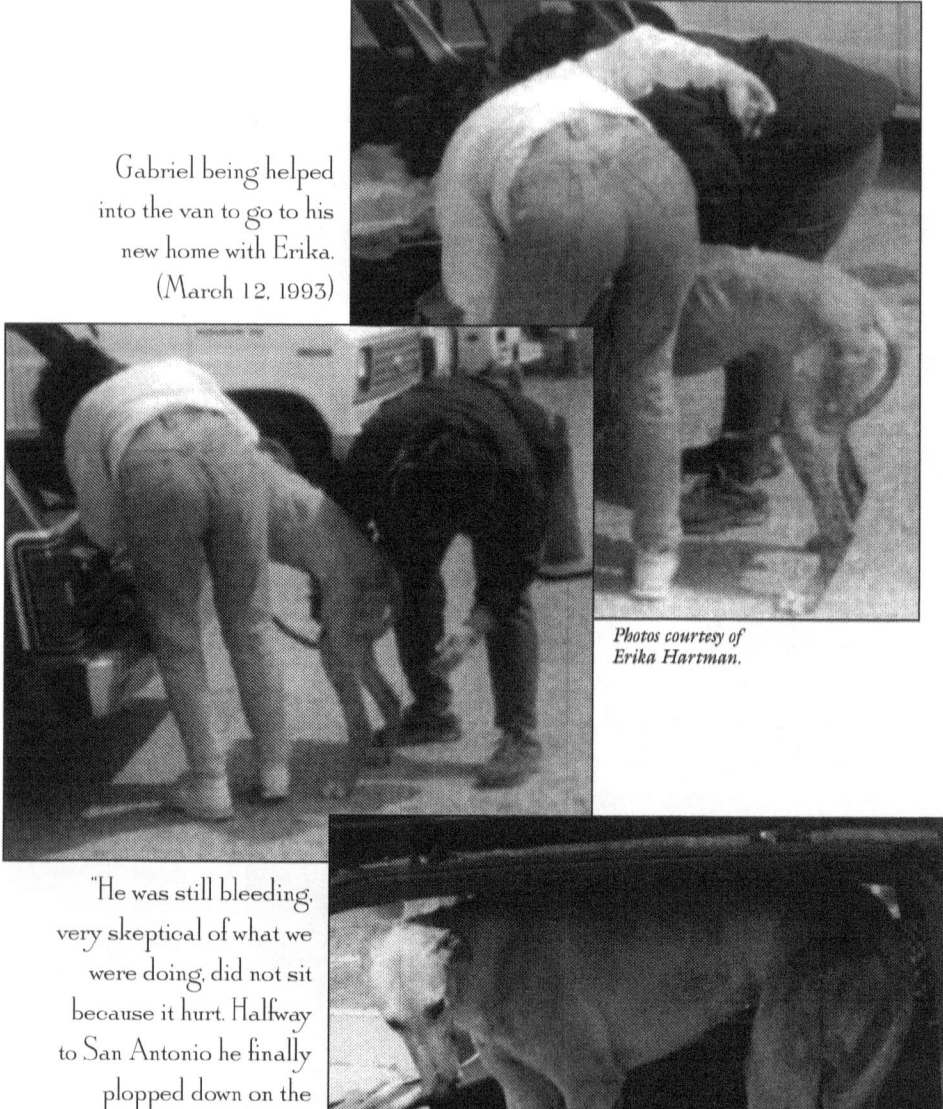

Gabriel being helped into the van to go to his new home with Erika. (March 12, 1993)

Photos courtesy of Erika Hartman.

"He was still bleeding, very skeptical of what we were doing, did not sit because it hurt. Halfway to San Antonio he finally plopped down on the comforter. He was very distrustful of me. I kept speaking to him in soft tones, telling him that all will be OK now."

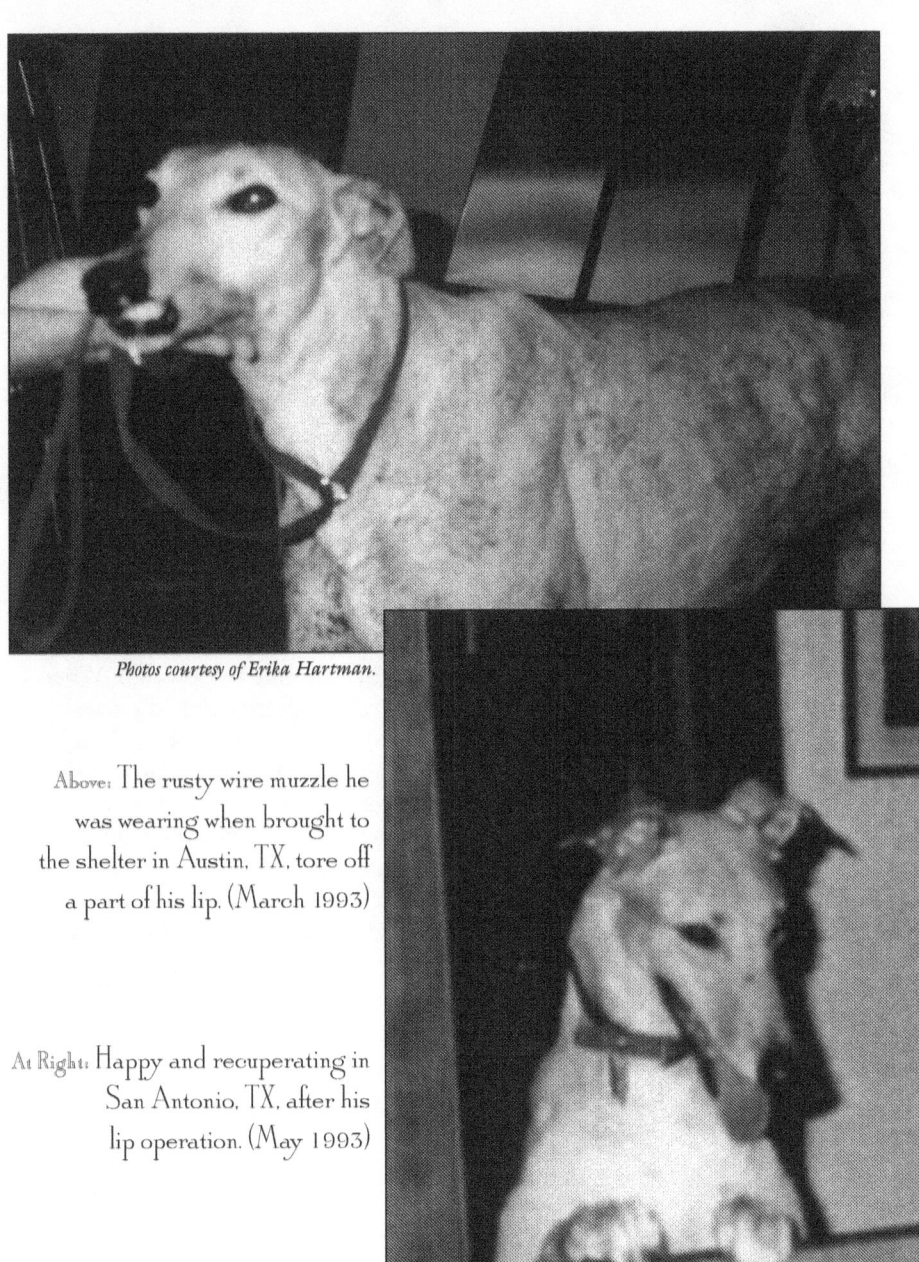

Photos courtesy of Erika Hartman.

Above: The rusty wire muzzle he
was wearing when brought to
the shelter in Austin, TX, tore off
a part of his lip. (March 1993)

At Right: Happy and recuperating in
San Antonio, TX, after his
lip operation. (May 1993)

"GABRIEL"

To my best friend, constant companion, my love, my Gabriel:

On Saturday, January 2, 2002, at 1:30 PM, your precious life was terminated. My heart has been broken once again, this time into many pieces. It was all too sudden. It started so plausible, an elderly dog developing arthritis, or so I thought. A little difficulty getting up, a moan and groan every now and then when sitting down. I thought an Adequan injection would help; it worked for some of my other dogs. Lillie is on her second injection and appears improved. But when Dr. Geannellis examined you, he suggested an X-ray of your left back hip joint. He said greyhounds develop problems in that area due to making fast turns to the left at the racetrack, which puts a lot of stress on that particular joint. Due to New Year's Eve and the new year coming up, the X-ray was postponed until January 2nd. By that time I knew severe pain had set in because you cried and whimpered all through the night.

I brought you to the clinic in the morning and in the late afternoon I received a phone call to come to the clinic. This was not a good sign. When I arrived, I was taken to a room where the X-ray was already tacked up and I was shown a walnut-sized tumor on your left back hip joint. I was told it was osteo-sarcoma! Bone cancer! I was stunned, and asked what the prognosis was, already knowing what I'd hear. Make him comfortable, etc., etc. I decided to bring you home and we started with pain killers, strong ones. One pill a day as prescribed wasn't enough, so I gave you two more, and the next night three of them plus tranquilizers. You were either in a drug-induced coma-like sleep, or in great pain once the medication wore off. So three days after the X-ray was taken, I made the horrific decision of euthanasia.

No matter how often I tell myself it was for the best, I feel so guilty, and yet I did not want you to suffer. I wanted you well so that we could go for long walks again and I could hug your body and I wanted you to peer out the window and bark at everything that moved. Fate intervened and took you from me.

Good bye, my beautiful, gregarious buddy! Till we meet again. Your loving care-giver,

– Erika

Bennington, VT
(January 7, 2002)

GREYHOUND RACING: THE FACTS

NATIONAL SCENE

- As of August 2001, 46 operating greyhound tracks are conducting live greyhound racing in 15 states [19 tracks operate seasonally, 27 operate year round.]

- The racing states and number of tracks in each are: Alabama (3), Arizona (3), Arkansas (1), Colorado (3), Connecticut (2), Florida (16), Iowa (2), Kansas (2), Massachusetts (2), New Hampshire (3), Oregon (1), Rhode Island (1), Texas (3), West Virginia (2), and Wisconsin (2).

- Seven states have banned live and/or simulcast greyhound racing since 1993. They are: Maine (1993), Virginia (1995), Vermont (1995), Idaho (1996), Washington (1996), Nevada (1997) and North Carolina (1998*).

- Based on recently published reports (August 2001), the dog racing industry continues to decline dramatically. According to industry statistics, dog racing held only a 0.7% share of the entire $61.6 billion annual U.S. gambling market in 2000, a decline of 6.65% or $32.6 million from 1999.

- The nation's two newest tracks, Shoreline Star in Connecticut and Camptown in Kansas, both of which opened in 1995, went bankrupt within one year or less. Shoreline reopened as a seasonal track in 1998. Camptown, which reopened in August 2000 as a seasonal track, closed 13 weeks later. A third track, Valley Park in Texas, closed since 1995, reopened for simulcasting in 2000. A three-month live racing seasonal resumed in December.

- Economic decline has forced the closure or the end of live racing at 16 dog tracks since 1991. Thirteen of the 16 are completely closed, including two that have been demolished, and three remain open for simulcasting only.

- State revenues from pari-mutuel dog racing have declined significantly from 1990-1998 (latest figures available).Some examples: Kansas[-59%], Arizona [-68%], Massachusetts [-69%], Oregon [-70%], Florida [-71%], Connecticut [-79%] and New Hampshire [-84%].

  * Live dog racing was outlawed in NC in 1954

GREYHOUND NUMBERS

- According to industry breeding reports published in *The Greyhound Review*, 77,852 litters were registered by the National Greyhound Association between 1989 and 2000. Multiplying these litters by a [low] average of 6.52 pups per litter results in a minimum total of 507,596 greyhounds born in this twelve-year period.

- Greyhounds are tattooed by three months of age and individually registered by 18 months. Of the 507,596 born, only 395,545 were individually registered — a discrepancy of 112,051 [22%] of puppies and young dogs that were culled [killed] from the system before the age of 18 months. Because rescue of young farm dogs is extremely rare, these culls are presumed dead.

- A comparison of the published numbers against the estimated combined number of dogs that are still racing (40,000), alive on breeding or training farms (30,000), and dogs that have been adopted (113,000), indicates that more than 325,000 greyhounds, including the culled puppies, have died between 1989 and 2000.

- On average, a revolving baseline of 1,000 dogs is needed to sustain a racetrack operation. As dogs grade off due to injury, age or poor performance, they must be continually replaced by a new population.

- Between 1971-1990 the number of operating tracks doubled to 56. This rapid expansion fueled a two-decade breeding frenzy that produced approximately 450,000 greyhounds in the 1980's alone.

- In 2000, approximately 26,500 greyhounds entered the racing system, and an equal or greater number of greyhounds, aged between 2 and 5 years old, exited the system. Approximately 13,000 "retired" dogs were rescued and adopted. An estimated 19,000 greyhounds were killed in 2000. This number includes 7,600 farm culls and 11,400 "retirees" that were not rescued.

- This "sport" has conservatively claimed the lives of more than 1,000,000 greyhounds in its 75-year U.S. history.

Prepared by *Greyhound Network News* and Greyhound Protection League   Revised August 2001

Page courtesy of GREYHOUND NETWORK NEWS
and GREYHOUND PROTECTION LEAGUE
(Revised Aug. 2001)

Racetrack Injury Reports

[Editors Note: The following information was compiled from greyhound injury reports obtained under public records requests from the racing commissions of Texas, West Virginia, and Wisconsin.]

Texas

Between Nov. 1, 2000 and June 15, 2001, a total of 728 greyhounds were injured while racing at the state's three tracks. The injury reports are broken down into nine generalized categories. With the exception of two dogs, no disposition was reported for the dogs that sustained serious injury. The less serious injuries or illness reported included gastrointestinal and respiratory problems, and "unknown."

Of the 420 greyhounds injured at **Gulf Greyhound Park**, one dog was euthanized by the track vet; two dogs sustained "catastrophic" injuries and were listed as "probable euthanasia." In all, 163 dogs sustained major injuries, many of which were career ending or required surgery.

Of the 225 greyhounds injured at **Corpus Christi Greyhound Track**, one dog was euthanized by the track vet; two dogs sustained "catastrophic" injuries and were listed as "probable euthanasia." In all, 68 dogs sustained major injuries, many of which were career ending or required surgery.

At **Valley Race Park**, 83 greyhounds were injured during the track's brief 12-week live racing season. Two dogs sustained "catastrophic" injuries and were listed as "probable euthanasia." An additional 45 dogs sustained major injuries requiring surgery.

West Virginia

Between October 2000 and April 2001, a total of 488 greyhounds were injured at **Tri-State Racetrack and Gaming Center**. Seventy-one greyhounds suffered bone fractures, including 37 hocks (tarsals), 11 quarter bones (metatarsals/metacarpals), 19 toes (phalanges), and three stopperbones (accessory carpals). One greyhound suffered a double long bone fracture of the front leg (radius and ulna). Four dogs were euthanized due to their injuries.

Included among the remaining injuries were 182 cramped or torn muscles and 71 lacerations.

The track veterinarian included the following paragraph — in bold face type — in each of her monthly summary reports to the racing commission: "As I have been saying since at least May of 1999, the track conditions must improve and become consistent on a race to race and day to day basis or we will continue to cripple dogs at an alarming rate."

Between November 2000 and May 2001, a total of 176 greyhounds were injured at **Wheeling Downs**. Of the total, 38 dogs suffered fractured hocks and two sustained long bone fractures. Twenty-eight of the injuries were categorized as "career ending," but no disposition was reported.

Three dogs suffered seizures — one had cluster seizures in the kennel, one had a seizure in the ginny pit (pre-race holding area), and one had a Grand Mal seizure following a race [disposition unknown]. One trainer reported May 27: "acute death when dog was returned to the kennel immediately following the race." Another greyhound died following a race in December, but no details were reported.

Wisconsin

The following injury statistics for the state's three greyhound tracks cover the seven-month period between November 2000 and May 2001 and include injuries incurred during official races, unofficial schooling races, and injuries reported by trainers:

A total of 152 greyhounds were injured at **Dairyland Greyhound Park**. Of the total, 31 were serious injuries, including 24 fractured hocks, four quarter bone and two long bone injuries, and one spinal injury.

A total of 108 greyhounds were injured at the **Geneva Lakes Greyhound Track**. Of the total, 43 were serious injuries, including 31 fractured hocks, seven quarter bone and four long bone injuries, and one spinal injury.

A total of 62 greyhounds were injured at the now-closed **St. Croix Meadows Greyhound Park**. Of the total, 10 were serious, including six fractured hocks and four quarter bone injuries.

There was no disposition recorded for the greyhounds with serious injuries. These injuries are usually considered to be career ending.

Racetrack Injury Reports

[*Editor's Note:* The following injury reports were obtained from the Colorado State Racing Commission under a public records request. Judy Kody Paulsen, director of Greyhound Companions of New Mexico, volunteered for the difficult task of deciphering these confusing and often misleading reports.]

Cloverleaf Kennel Club: In the 17-week period ending June 5, 2001, a total of 56 injuries were confirmed by the track vet. Those injuries included 27 fractures, 16 muscle and ligament injuries, and 11 unspecified injuries. [Commission's numbers do not agree]. An additional 41 injuries were reported by trainers but were not confirmed by the track vet.

Mile High Kennel Club: In the 17-week period ending Feb. 4, 2001, a total of 51 injuries were confirmed by the track vet. Those injuries included 22 fractures and dislocations, 12 muscle and ligament injuries, and 17 unspecified injuries. An additional 39 injuries were reported by trainers but were not confirmed by the track vet.

Pueblo Greyhound Park: In the 26-week period ending July 1, 2001, a total of 50 injuries were confirmed by the track vet. Those injuries included 30 fractures and dislocations, 12 muscle and ligament injuries, and eight unspecified injuries. An additional 32 injuries were reported by trainers but were not confirmed by the track vet.

Racetrack Injury Reports copied from GREYHOUND NETWORK NEWS *with permission.*

Top Report: WINTER 2001-02.

Bottom Report: SUMMER 2001.

Racetrack Injury Reports

[*Editor's Note:* The following information was compiled from 275 individual greyhound injury reports from The Woodlands, Wichita, and Camptown greyhound tracks in Kansas. The reports were obtained from the Kansas Racing and Gaming Division under a public records request.]

Anatomical index of bone fracture sites referred to below:

Long bones: the humerus, radius, and ulna, bones of the foreleg and the femur, tibia, and fibula, bones of the hind leg. **Carpus:** wrist joint on the foreleg. **Tarsus:** hock joint on the hind leg. **Metacarpals:** the bones of the forefoot. **Metatarsals:** the bones of the hind foot.

A total of 173 greyhounds racing at **The Woodlands** were injured in 2000. Of the total, two dogs suffered spinal injuries and three had long bone fractures. There were 40 tarsal injuries, 34 of them fractures. One report noted, "audible 'pop' of hock in center of first turn, carried off." Nine of these dogs were euthanized.

Fifteen dogs suffered metatarsal injuries, nine of which were fractures. Four dogs suffered tail fractures, seven had carpal injuries, 15 had metatarsal injuries, and 12 had toe injuries. Fifty-three dogs suffered pulled, torn, dropped, or cramped muscles. A cramp injury on a 66-pound, 3-year-old female was described as a "whole body cramp."

Two greyhounds were injured by the lure. A 60-pound, 21-month-old female was injured during the evening performance May 26. The injury report noted, "dog got into rail at brake. Current was on. Dog shocked but removed from rail alive and responsive." During a matinee performance on Aug. 13, a 68-pound, 17-month-old male was "hit by lure — skull abrasion — left front thorax — lure hit left side and front leg."

The remaining 30 injuries included lacerations, abrasions, sprains, and split webs.

A total of 81 greyhounds were injured in 2000 at **Wichita Greyhound Park.** Eight dogs suffered long bone fractures; three were euthanized. One dog suffered a hip joint fracture.

Twenty-three dogs suffered tarsal fractures; one was euthanized. There were three carpal fractures, eight metatarsal fractures, and five broken toes. Twenty dogs suffered muscle injuries. The remaining 13 injuries included lacerations, dislocated toes, and sprains.

There were 21 injuries reported at **Camptown Greyhound Park** during its brief resumption of live racing between Aug. 4 and Nov. 14, 2000. Ten greyhounds suffered tarsal fractures; seven were euthanized. Two dogs suffered long bone fractures; both were euthanized. Two dogs suffered metatarsal fractures; one was euthanized. One greyhound suffered a carpal fracture and was euthanized. The remaining six dogs suffered torn or strained muscles.

Chapter 9. The Disappeared Ones

O'Fallon is the small city outside of St. Louis, MO, where the decayed and dying bodies of former racers were found.

According to Amnesty International USA, active and outspoken defenders of human rights from all walks of life have been arrested, tortured, and murdered by their respective governments. According to this human rights organization, the countries are India, Tunisia, Nigeria, West Africa, Haiti, Syria, Turkey, China and Brazil.

This writer first learned about The Disappeared Ones many years ago. At that time persons living in some countries of South America were being abducted (and still are) and were never seen or heard from again. Among them were not just dissidents, but ordinary persons who were suspect because they were friends or acquaintances or relatives (including young children) of the dissidents.

Chapter 10. Fire
(the kennel compound in Lynn, MA)

According to reporter Marie Lingblom, as of March 1999, license records of the city of Lynn indicated there were about 1,662 racers housed in this compound, which includes twenty-six different kennels. They are made of wood. (*Source:* North Shore Sunday, 9-12-99.)

As anticipated, a fourth fire occurred at this compound on June 18, 1999, which claimed the lives of eight racers. It was caused by human error when some one plugged in the heating unit that is used in the whirlpool bath, and forgot to place it in the water. It reportedly lay on the wooden floor near some newspapers and rags, which caught fire. It also was reported that all of the dogs had been removed from the kennel building, but eight ran back and perished. This would not have happened had an automatic sprinkler system been in place. In Massachusetts, sprinkler systems aren't mandated in kennels.

Few persons are aware of the 1986 and 1990 fires. Twenty-eight racers perished in the former and none in the latter. A few days after the 1999 fire, Massachusetts Citizens Against Dog Racing started a letter writing campaign and the following month a petition drive was started asking Governor Paul Cellucci and Lynn mayor Patrick McManus to condemn and close the Lynn compound which is quite old, in poor condition, and a fire hazard. Both the letter writing campaign and petition drive were unsuccessful.

Libby Frattaroli and Greyhound advocates at the kennel compound in Lynn, MA. after the fourth fire in June 1999.

Photo courtesy of Libby Frattaroli.

Chapter 11. We're Nobody's Property
(slaughterhouses and more)

In an interview in 1971, Franz Stangl, Commandant of Treblinka and Sobibor death camps, recalled the following at the Belzec death camp in 1942: "I can't describe to you what it was like ... the smell, oh God, the smell, it was everywhere ... not hundreds, thousands of corpses ... Oh God. That's where Wirth (Christian Wirth, Stangl's superior) told me that was what Sobibor was for, and that he was putting me officially in charge... When I was on a trip years later in Brazil, my train stopped next to a slaughterhouse. The cattle in the pens were very close to my window, one crowding the other, looking at me through that fence. I thought ... this reminds me of Poland, that's just how people looked, trustingly just before they went into the tins." (*Source:* Response, Winter 1999/2000, p. 7. Response is a publication of the Simon Wiesenthal Center, 9760 West Pico Blvd., Los Angeles, CA 90035. The Center tracks down Holocaust murderers so that justice may be served. It is also a passionate advocate for human rights.)

AUTHOR'S NOTE: Could this happen again? The world is ablaze with hate and I belive it could. Sadly, I belive it could.

In a story by Isaac Bashevis Singer, one of the characters comments that what the Nazis did to the Jewish people, humans do to animals every day.

According to one New York newspaper, "Rodney King, the African-American motorist beaten by police, testified yesterday that he felt like an animal waiting to be slaughtered as he lay bound and bloodied in the final moments of the attack." King said that during the March 3, 1991, beating he felt "like a cow that was waiting to be slaughtered – just like a piece of meat." In a federal trial, two of the four police officers were found guilty of violating Mr. King's civil rights and are serving thirty-month sentences. (*Source:* The New York Post, Tuesday, March 29, 1994.)

Be aware that when humans torture and murder other humans, whether they be slaves, captives of war, women, political dissidents, or others, they rationalize that the victims are no better than "animals."

Humans brand cows and calves on their faces with red hot irons without anesthesia, and the Nazi did the same on the arms of Jewish victims. Humans surgically remove the ovaries of cows destined for slaughter without anesthesia, and in some parts of the world it is custom/tradition to genitally mutilate women, likewise without anesthesia.

The following two cases reinforce the position that animals of other species are more than just somebody's property:

In a recent cat custody case before the Arlington County, Virginia, Circuit Court, the judge said he would decide "what is in the best interest of Grady…". From what I have seen, Grady would be better off with Mr. Zovko. (*Source:* The Animals' Advocate, newsletter of the Animal Legal Defense Fund, Petaluna, CA, Spring 2000, p. 4.)

In another state, the judge set aside that part of a deceased person's will that called for the destruction of his surviving animal. (*Source:* The Animals' Advocate, newsletter of the Animal Legal Defense Fund, Petaluna, CA, Spring 2000, p. 4.)

Human Property

In the New York Post (December 13, 1993), in an article titled "Asia – Arab World scandal: Millions of child slaves," Jean Kirkpatrick discusses an article written by Robert Senser in the December 1993, issue of Freedom Review. She informs us that Mr. Senser advised it's been estimated that more than 200 million children, ages eight to fourteen, work twelve to fourteen hour days, seven days a week, under subhuman conditions for pennies or nothing. The countries involved are Bangladesh, India, Pakistan, Nepal and China. He reports that the children are either lured or tricked into leaving home, and then are beaten, raped and enslaved.

According to Ms. Kirkpatrick, Mr. Senser advises that entire export companies depend upon child bondage, and in India alone, it's been estimated that fifty-five million children are held in bondage. In addition, Mr. Senser reports that governments and international officials for the most part have refused to condemn this slavery and brutality.

In another publication it was reported that "slavery is making a comeback" in Mauritania and the Sudan where Arab militias, armed by the government of Sudan, raid villages, killing the men and enslaving the women and children. The latter either are kept by their captors or sold, many of them at auctions. Some are castrated, some hobbled – their Achilles tendons are cut, and some are branded. (*Source:* from a report given by Charles Jacobs and Mohamed Athie of the American Anti-Slavery Group, as reported in Animal People, October 1994, p. 18.)

Animal People is a must newspaper for people who care about animals; in other words who are animal people. Its address is: Animal People, P.O. Box 960, Clinton WA 98236-9903. The editor and publisher are, respectively, Merritt Clifton and Kim Bartlett.

In some countries, women are still considered commodities and the property of their husbands or parents. In Pakistan, for instance, it's been reported that hundreds of women are murdered each year in the name of honor. Many more murders occur but go unreported. In Pakistan and other countries in the same part of the world, women are expected to submit to their husbands and fathers and live passive lives in seclusion. When they attempt to assert themselves, they're murdered. Recently in Pakistan, a young mother of two children was shot to death in her attorney's office. She was planning to file for divorce from an abusive husband. It's been alleged that her parents instigated her murder as a matter of honor because she was shaming them. It also has been reported that the authorities know the persons responsible for her murder, yet no charges have been brought against them. Her attorney, Hina Jilani and her female colleagues have been publicly condemned and threatened with death.

In the same part of the world women who report having been raped are also put to death in the name of honor because it's felt that they too have brought shame to their families and communities. And in those instances when the perpetrators of these "honor" killings are brought to trial, they receive sentences of a few months or perhaps a year in prison. (*Source:* Amnesty Now, publication of Amnesty International, USA, Winter 2000 and Spring 2000.)

Worldwide, women from the Ukraine, Mexico, Czechoslovakia, and other countries, including the United States, are being sold into slavery as sex slaves. Women's Rights activists say that if the world is to be safe for humanity, it must be safe for women too. Let's take this a few steps further; if the world is to be safe for humanity, it must be safe for all of its inhabitants: men, women, children, and animals of other species. In other words, it must be a safe place for all of us regardless of species.

(Below are excerpts from an Amnesty International USA letter of May 2, 2001. Reprinted here with permission.)

In 1996, a pregnant Kazal Khidhr was detained by her husband's relatives in Iraqi, Kurdistan. They accused her of extra-marital sex, cut off her nose and said they would kill her after the baby was born.

Fortunately, Kazal managed to escape before the death threat could be carried out. She found protection in a women's refuge in the city of Sulaimaniya. And, with the help of human rights activists, she eventually got out of the country and was granted asylum in a foreign land.

Torture in The Name of "Honor"

Women and girls are tortured in the name of honor around the world. They are accused of bringing shame on their families for behavior ranging from chatting with a male neighbor to having sexual relations outside of marriage.

Women on whom suspicion falls are punished in the belief that family members have no alternative but to remove the stain on their honor. Honor crimes range from beatings to disfiguration of the face, death by stoning and, amazingly, it is the women who are seen as the guilty party and the men who are seen as the victims since they have suffered a loss of honor.

But honor crimes can extend beyond the home. In many traditional societies, women who dare to demand a more empowered role in village life are subject to the same violence. Among the numerous countries reporting such honor crimes are Iraq, Jordan, Egypt, Pakistan and Turkey.

Abusing Women for Profit

Trafficking of human beings is the third largest source of profit for international organized crime, after drugs and arms, with revenue amounting to billions of dollars each year. The United Nations believes upwards of four million people – mostly women and children – are trafficked annually and that trafficking occurs in every part of the world.

Many women are recruited on false pretenses, coerced, transported and sold for a range of exploitative purposes. Some are trafficked into the sex industry, others into domestic labor. Trafficked women are subjected to a range of human rights violations including beatings, sexual assaults and other forms of torture.

Torture of Women in Prison

All too often, women who are imprisoned for any reason are subject to sexual abuse and other forms of torture at the hands of their guards and custodians. Tragically, the United States, which prides itself on abiding by the rule of law, doesn't always manage to do so.[1]

(End of AIUSA letter excerpts.)

Primum Non Nocere
First Do No Harm

– *Hippocrates*

The Hippocratic Oath tells the medical profession to
"First Do No Harm."

It is therefore highly probable that
Hippocrates would oppose animal research,
if not because of the harm it inflicts upon animals
of other species, then because of the harm
it inflicts upon human animals.

– The Author

Chapter 12. Animal Research:
Science Gone Mad
A Greyhound's Nightmare, Every Animal's Nightmare

In April 2000, federal authorities were looking for Daniel Shonka, a kennel *owner* who, while operating a racing kennel at the St. Croix Meadows dog track in Hudson, WI, duped kennel operators in Illinois and nearby states into thinking he'd find homes for their retired Greyhounds. Instead, he illegally sold them to research laboratories. At the time, he was a member of the National Greyhound Association, ran a Greyhound adoption group from his home in Iowa, and had a Class B dealers license from the U.S. Department of Agriculture, which permitted him to sell dogs to research facilities.

These former racers, however, were sold illegally, most of them to a cardiac research lab in Minnesota that manufactures implantable pacemakers and defibrillators. These are painful and terminal experiments, and as of June 2000, 1,086 Greyhounds were traced to that one lab. Mr. Shonka sold the dogs for $400 each, and state gaming officials estimated he made about $500,000 in three years. It's important to remember he told the racers' *owners* that he was placing them for adoption.

The scam was uncovered by the detective work of two women: Sherry Cotner, North Carolina representative of the GPL, and Cynthia Cash, another Greyhound advocate. After the intervention of an attorney retained by the GPL, the lab agreed to surgically reverse the procedures on those dogs who were still alive. They had scars on their necks, which had been shaved and through which lead wires had been inserted into their jugular veins and then into their hearts. As of late June 2000, fifty-six Greyhounds had been released after the two women identified and contacted their *owners* who, as already noted, thought their dogs had been placed for adoption. By the end of May 2000, the legal fees totaled $8,000. They were paid by the GPL, which assumed responsibility for paying the additional fees that were anticipated. (*Source:* GNN, Summer 2000, pp. 1, 3 and 8.)

At a hearing on October 7, 2000, the National Greyhound Association Board of Directors revoked Dan Shonka's membership and privileges for having sold or placed Greyhounds into research facilities without the permission of their *owners* of record. (*Source:* The Greyhound Review, December 2000.)

In June 1999, the Mississippi State Supreme Court reinstated a suit brought against Mississippi State University to release Greyhounds who had been donated for research purposes. It was believed persons at a dog track that had closed had donated the racers. (*Source:* In Defense of Animals Magazine, Fall, 1999, p. 9.)

In June 1998, Colorado State University said it no longer would use live Greyhounds in its terminal teaching labs for future veterinarians. But at CSU's request, the following year a bill was introduced into the state legislature asking that its records be closed to the public. It was passed by the state House and Senate and signed into law by the governor. (*Source:* GNN, Fall 1998.)

Of the 2,652 racers used at CSU for dissection purposes and terminal labs between 1995 and 1998, 214 were donated by Massachusetts-licensed *owners* and kennel *owners*. (*Source:* New England Anti Vivisection Society, 333 Washington St., Suite 850, Boston, Massachusetts 02108. Its source was Rocky Mountain News.)

In the Autumn 2000, issue of Good Medicine, it was reported that the vice president and CEO of Denver's Channel 7 (an affiliate of station ABC) repeatedly broadcast the following editorial:

"Every year CU (Colorado State University) medical students operate on live dogs to see how their organs react to drugs – most often heart and kidney drugs. The dogs are anesthetized, operated on, and then killed. These dog labs, costing more than $40,000 each, are supported with your tax dollars. The CU School of Medicine says this lab experience is invaluable. But we believe, along with many students and other medical schools, that this practice is barbaric. Harvard, Yale, Columbia and Stanford medical schools, along with seventy others, have abolished these labs and replaced them with computer simulations or human surgery observations. Channel 7 calls on Richard Krugman, dean of CU's medical school, to close the dog labs. Stop this unethical practice and bring CU into the 21st century."

Good Medicine is a publication of the Physicians' Committee for Responsible Medicine (PCRM). Its address is: Good Medicine, 5100 Wisconsin Avenue NW – Suite 400, Washington DC 20016.

Between February 1994 and April 1997, 595 racers were donated to Iowa State University for research purposes. Of this number, 502 racers were donated by five members of the National Greyhound Association (NGA). (*Source:* GNN, Fall 1999.)

Between January 1996 and May 1998, 111 Greyhounds were donated to Kansas State University. Fifty-four were adults and fifty-seven were puppies. Two of the adults were adopted and the remaining 109 adults and puppies were put to death. Ten females were nursing, and they and their puppies were put to death after the puppies were weaned. The Greyhounds were donated by a variety of kennels in Kansas. (*Source:* GNN, Winter 1998/1999.)

Great Apes

In October 1999, the New Zealand Parliament passed a law prohibiting the use of great apes in testing, research or education for the benefit of humans. Included are chimpanzees, bonobos, gorillas and orangutans. This is the first time that the status of great apes has been recognized in legislation. (*Source:* The Animals Agenda, P.O. Box 25881, Baltimore, MD 21224, January/February 2000, and Bridging The Gap, newsletter of The Great Ape Project International, Autumn/Winter 1999.)

Gibbons, are considered small apes and they too are used in painful and terminal research in the U.S. Shirley McGreal, founder and chairwoman of the International Primate Protection League (IPPL) in Summerville, SC, writes, "They are the smallest of the apes and excel in acrobatics. They sing beautiful songs, which carry for long distances." (*Source:* IPPL News, April 2001.)

Unfortunately, since 1986, the National Institutes of Health (NIH) has spent about $50 million to breed chimpanzees at five laboratories. But because fewer chimpanzees are being used in experiments (for both ethical and scientific reasons), there now is a large "surplus" of laboratory chimpanzees. These great apes think, feel and behave much like humans; they speak their own languages, use tools, and make moral choices as do humans. Unless the Federal government provides the funding to place them in sanctuaries, they'll be condemned to live out the remainder of their lives in solitary confinement in small, barren cages. Chimpanzees can live up to fifty years. (*Source:* In Defense of Animals (IDA), 131 Camino Alto, Suite E, Mill Valley, CA 94941.)

In August 1999, The Coulston Foundation (TCF) signed an unusual legal agreement with the U.S. Department of Agriculture (USDA), in which it was forced to surrender 300 of its 650 chimpanzees and make improvements in its facility located in New Mexico. Since 1994, In Defense of Animals (IDA) has been in the forefront of this battle and it was the first time that a research laboratory was forced to give up any of its animals as well as adhere to severe restrictions and oversight measures. This is an indication of the horrendous conditions there.

For more than five years, IDA provided the USDA with documentary evidence obtained from whistle-blowers and its own investigators. The USDA charged TCF with a variety of violations of the Animal Welfare Act, including the deaths of six chimpanzees, one of whom had been used in invasive spinal cord experiments (his spinal cord had been severed). Yet it's a scientific fact that deliberately paralyzing an animal of another species cannot lead to a treatment for human paraplegics.

The IDA is insisting that not just 300, but all 650 chimpanzees be retired to sanctuaries. It also is calling for a moratorium on experiments that infect them with infectious diseases such as HIV and hepatitis; it's not easy to find sanctuaries for infected animals. IDA also is seeking government funding for the retirement of TCF chimpanzees as well as others who no longer are being used for research purposes but who are living in deplorable conditions, including being caged in solitary confinement in federally funded laboratories. As already noted, IDA reports that since 1986, the federal government has spent over $50 million breeding chimpanzees for research purposes in the U.S. Surely the government should assume responsibility to pay for their retirement. (*Source:* IDA Magazine, Fall 1999, pp. 2 and 3.)

After the National Institutes of Health confiscated the approximately 300 chimpanzees from The Coulston Foundation, it decided to give responsibility for their long-term care to Charles River Laboratories, reportedly one of the world's largest dealers, breeders, and importers of nonhuman primates. This means they'll be used for research purposes just as they would have been had they remained at TCF. In addition, the NIH was planning to buy fourteen infant chimpanzees from The Coulston Foundation at a cost of $400,000 and ship them to another research laboratory. (*Source:* IDA letter, June 14, 2001.)

It would appear that the National Institutes of Health is bailing out The Coulston Foundation in the amount of $400,000 in taxpayer monies and at the same time is condemning these tiny infants to a lifetime of hell.

UPDATE: It has been reported that as of July 2001, the NIH cancelled all funding of TCF primate lab in Alamogordo, NM. (*Source:* The Animals Agenda, p. 32, September/October, 2001.) *And according to IDA, a bank in New Mexico has filed foreclosure papers against Frederick Coulston and TCF, and the latter appears to be on the brink of bankruptcy. IDA has worked for seven years to accomplish this and if it does happen, there will be one less lab testing pesticides, fungicides, insecticides, toxic chemicals, drugs and spinal devices on chimpanzees and monkeys. For more information, contact IDA.*

Chimpanzees are almost 99% genetically identical to us, so one could say that experimenting on them is the same thing as experimenting on us. This little more than 1% DNA difference, however, makes them invalid models for us. Chimpanzees don't naturally contract the human AIDS virus, and in spite of the research industry's attempts to artificially infect them with it, they just don't get it. They don't contract the disease. Dr. Jane Goodall, known for her decades of studying chimpanzees in their own environments, has said that ever since the early 1980s, researchers have been injecting the human AIDS virus into chimpanzees' brains, spinal cords, blood and muscles, and they haven't contracted it.

She advises that Robert Gallo now says that chimpanzees are useless in AIDS research. At present he is the director of the University of Maryland's Institute of Human Virology, but once was associated with the National Institutes of Health, the agency responsible for funding Aids and all other research, much of it animal research, in the U.S. (*Source:* Interview with Dr. Jane Goodall, Modern Maturity, November/December 1999, pp. 25, 26, 27.)

It certainly appears that chimpanzees don't naturally contract HIV. And even though they're artificially infected with the virus, they don't show symptoms of or become ill with the disease. Jerom is the one possible exception. Not long ago, a variety of HIV strains was injected into a group of chimpanzees. It is believed that they must have mutated in Jerom. He died. He died at fourteen. Researchers then took fluid from Jerom and and injected it into other chimpanzees, none of whom to date have become ill. Precious Jerom no longer is living in hell, but so many, many others are. Please go to: *www.lpag.org.*

Since chimpanzees can live up to fifty years, those who are infected/tainted with the human aids virus as well as other infectious and deadly human viruses, must live out the remainder of their lives alone, in solitary confinement, in barren, steel cages. In their cages these sociable, intelligent, almost-persons rock back and forth, mutilate themselves, and live miserable lives of unseen and quiet desperation. What is being done to them nation and worldwide is truly beyond understanding.

Until the research community acknowledges that animal research is wrong from both a scientific and ethical perspective, it will refuse to use human cell, tissue and organ cultures, and will not participate in human clinical studies. It will continue experimenting on animals of other species. But vivisection does not and can not save human lives. If we're ever to put an end to animal research and the horrendous pain and suffering it inflicts on all of us, we must reach and touch not just the minds of researchers, but their hearts as well.[2]

Alternatives to Animal Labs: There appears to be a trend to offer alternatives to painful and terminal animal labs.

In the fall of 2001, a new veterinary medical school, Western University College of Veterinary Medicine in Pomona, CA, will open its doors. It will be totally committed to using animals only in ways that will benefit them. Lara Rasmussen, D.V.M., developed a willed body program so that students may work on cadavers that have been ethically obtained. In addition, she is working with a manufacturer to design animal models of large animals (such as cows and horses) that are anatomically accurate for student use. It's to be hoped that more and more veterinary colleges will do likewise. (*Source:* New England Anti-Vivisection Society, (NEAVS), March 2000, 333 Washington St., Suite 850, Boston, MA 02108.)

Johns Hopkins University in Baltimore, MD, and Wake Forest University in Winston Salem, NC, have eliminated all animal labs from medical school classes. (*Source:* Physicians' Committee for Responsible Medicine, May 2000.)

On February 9, 2000, NEAVS and Tufts University School of Veterinary Medicine issued a joint statement in the Worcester Telegram and Gazette announcing that Tufts was ending its terminal dog lab as an elective for third year veterinary students. The article reported, "Tufts' decision comes after years of pressure and protests from students – only twelve signed up for the third-year (elective) course this year – and, more recently, an aggressive campaign by the New England Anti-Vivisection Society, which worked to move Tufts toward cruelty-free veterinary training." Tufts now is the first of our country's twenty-seven veterinary schools to announce plans to eliminate terminal animal labs where healthy animals are used and then put to death at the end of the class. (*Source:* NEAVS.)

During the past several years the Association of Veterinarians for Animal Rights (AVAR) in Davis, CA, has convinced a number of veterinary medical schools to offer students alternative methods of teaching that aren't invasive or lethal, and to drop terminal surgery labs.

In December 1999, the Israeli Minister of Education, Yossi Sarid, banned animal experimentation in schools. He said dissection isn't necessary for education, and that it's more important to teach children compassion for animals. (*Source:* Good Medicine, Winter 2000, p. 23; a publication of PCRM.)

In the 1980s, researchers at the American Museum of Natural History in New York City blinded, deafened and mutilated the sex organs of cats and kittens in order to learn how these invasive procedures would affect their sexual performance. Surely this perversion of science can not benefit animals of any species. It took many years of demonstrations and massive amounts of publicity by the late Henry Spira and others before federal funding for this horrendous research finally was stopped.

It's unreasonable to expect to find a cure for human animals by artificially inducing a human disease in other-specied animals, then looking for a cure for that artificially induced disease and then applying the findings to humans. It just doesn't work. We're too different in too many different ways – anatomically as well as physiologically and metabolically. Since older and younger humans react differently to the same drugs and chemicals, and since different species of animals react differently to the same drugs and chemicals, the reactions between them and us to the same drugs and chemicals are even more pronounced. Penicillin and aspirin are fatal to some other-specied animals. And whereas morphine acts as a depressant in humans, it stimulates horses. As for penicillin, it was put on hold for about ten years because it failed to effectively treat systemic infections in rabbits. How senseless and sad that large numbers of human and other-specied animals died because rabbits didn't respond to penicillin. On the other hand, many drugs that have tested safe on animals of other species have killed or seriously harmed humans.

One of many examples is the diabetes drug Rezulin, which caused severe liver damage in humans, but had tested safe in laboratory animals. It was removed from the market. (*Source:* Good Medicine, Autumn 2000.) Another example is tobacco. Lab animals who are forced to inhale tobacco smoke don't contract cancer. Yet we know that tobacco causes cancer in humans. On the other hand, some products that cause tumors in lab animals are safe for humans, such as Saccharin. (*Source:* PCRM, Sept. 5, 2002.) It would appear from the evidence that animal testing is medically and scientifically invalid for human purposes; likewise as a basis for environmental laws and regulations. Animal research is a multi-million dollar industry that wastes taxpayer dollars and the lives of human animals and animals of other species.

In the 1970s, the U.S. government declared a War on Cancer. Yet almost thirty years later this war hasn't been won. Many suspect it's because there has been too much emphasis on and funding for animal research. For instance, animal researchers deliberately induce or surgically implant malignant tumors in healthy animals of other species and then attempt to treat them by infusing them with a variety of toxic chemicals. But cancers develop spontaneously in humans; they're not deliberately induced. And because of the many differences between the species, it's misleading, harmful and deadly to all of us to apply the findings from them to us.

It's an old myth that perpetuates vivisection/animal research. The late pediatrician, Dr. Robert Mendelsohn said, "The reason I am against animal research is because it doesn't work. It has no scientific value. One cannot extrapolate the results of animal research to human beings, and every good scientist knows that." (*Source:* Lethal Medicine, published by The Nature of Wellness, P.O. Box 10400, Glendale, CA 91209-3400.)

Dr. Moneim Fadali has written, "Animal models differ from their human counterparts. Conclusions drawn from animal research when applied to human disease delay progress, mislead and do harm to the patient." (*Source:* "Animal Experimentation, A Harvest of Shame," Hidden Springs Press, 1996.)

In their book, "Sacred Cows and Golden Geese: The Human Cost of Experiments on Animals," Ray Greek, M.D., and Jean Swingle Greek, D.V.M., also discuss the dangers of animal research to human health.

To find a cure for diseases in dogs, cats and other animals of different species, researchers don't experiment on human animals.

They know it doesn't make sense to do so. Well, the reverse is just as true. But in vitro tests (test tube cultures, etc.), computer simulators, and human clinical studies do make sense. They have been extremely successful in finding cures for human diseases. They're also faster (it takes many years before the results, often incorrect, of animal tests can be determined). They're far less expensive (animal research requires the spending of untold millions of dollars) and they do no harm. They do no harm to anyone. It should be noted that there are large numbers of persons suffering from deadly diseases who are willing to participate in non-invasive experimental treatment and drug testing. Finally, human gene studies are making animal research a disposable remnant of the Dark Ages.

As for cosmetics and household products, there is no law that requires they be tested on animals, and although about 500 companies no longer do so, some large, well-known companies continue to do so. (*Source:* IDA Magazine, Fall 1999, p. 11.)

Unfortunately, not many other-specied animals escape the scalpels, drugs, restraining devices, and other instruments of torture of the "killers in white coats," to quote Murphy's shelter buddy, Big Boy. Among them are mice, rats, ferrets, chinchillas, dogs, cats, rabbits, farm animals, equines, dolphins, elephants and nonhuman primates.

It was People for the Ethical Treatment of Animals (PETA) in Norfolk, VA, that first made the author aware of animal research and its horrors. PETA's undercover work has also exposed the cruelty of fur farms, animal "entertainment" and so much more. Likewise have many organizations and groups that haven't been mentioned.

Human Animals in Research

In a recent interview with Der Spiegel, a German newspaper, Hans Muench, now eighty-seven, said that he had no regrets about the experiments he conducted on Jewish inmates at Auschwitz during World War II. He also praised another Auschwitz doctor, the infamous Dr. Josef Mengele, who performed horrendously brutal and painful experiments on Jewish inmates. Muench even boasted, "I could conduct experiments on humans that otherwise are only possible on rabbits." (Source: Response, Winter-Spring 1999, p. 8; publication of the Simon Weisenthal Center.)

During World War II, the Japanese brutally experimented on innocent Asian civilians and Allied prisoners of war including Chinese, Koreans, Russians, and perhaps Americans. Yet the U.S. government granted all the perpetrators/war criminals blanket immunity in return for sharing the results of these experiments. (*Source:* Response, Winter/Spring, 1999, p. 2.)

For information about the heinous experiments conducted on U.S. military personnel since the 1940s, see the Staff Report that was prepared for the U.S. Senate's Committee on Veterans' Affairs, December 8, 1994, John D. Rockefeller IV (West Virginia), Chairman. It may be accessed via: *www.gulfwarvets.com/senate.htm.*

For information about experiments conducted on other human subjects, see Slaughter of the Innocent, by Hans Ruesch, Civitas Publications., and The Treatment, by Martha Stevens, Duke University Press, Durham, NC.

Photo courtesy of G.M.

Steve Baer (the tall one) and other primate advocates during a peaceful protest at the New England Regional Primate Center in Southboro, MA. (Sept. 1998)

ANIMAL EXPERIMENTATION HAS BECOME A BAD HABIT—ONE THAT IS OFTEN SCIENTIFICALLY UNNECESSARY, MEDICALLY UNRELIABLE, AND ALWAYS UNDENIABLY CRUEL.

ANIMALS ARE INDIVIDUALS WHO HAVE A VALUE INDEPENDENT OF THEIR USEFULNESS TO HUMANS.

Courtesy of Joseph Piroso.

Original artwork by the late Denise (Nee Cee) Piroso.

...Betrayal

From the time they are infants, they are raised by human hands. To gain their trust and love, they are held, hugged, played with and kissed ... totally unaware of the tragic fate that awaits them. At the "appropriate" age, they are sedated, injected and infected.

Many of these highly intelligent animals are given deadly diseases and isolated in cages not much larger than a bathroom stall, where they will spend countless days, months, or years unable to touch or hug another living being, their only contact being with masked technicians. When their research days are over, they are warehoused for the rest of their lives, which can span up to 60 years. Today, an estimated 1,700 chimpanzees live in six research centers throughout the U.S.

Brochure panel courtesy of IDA, reprinted with permission.

For more information, please contact:

In Defense of Animals
131 Camino Alto
Mill Valley, CA 94941
www.idausa.org

SIGN THE DECLARATION

A DECLARATION ON GREAT APES

We demand the extension of the community of equals to include all great apes: human beings, chimpanzees, gorillas, bonobos, and orang-utans.

The community of equals is the moral community within which we accept certain basic moral principles or rights as governing our relations with each other and enforceable at law. Among these principles or rights are the following:

1. The Right to Life
The lives of members of the community of equals are to be protected. Members of the community of equals may not be killed except in very strictly defined circumstances, for example, self-defense.

2. The Protection of Individual Liberty
Members of the community of equals are not to be arbitrarily deprived of their liberty; if they should be imprisoned without due legal process, they have the right to immediate release. The detention of those who have not been convicted of any crime, or of those who are not criminally liable, should be allowed only where it can be shown to be for their own good, or necessary to protect the public from a member of the community who would clearly be a danger to others if at liberty. In such cases, members of the community of equals must have the right to appeal, either directly or, if they lack the relevant capacity, through an advocate, to a judicial tribunal.

3. The Prohibition of Torture
The deliberate infliction of severe pain on a member of the community of equals, either wantonly or for an alleged benefit to others, is regarded as torture, and is wrong.

If you endorse The Declaration on Great Apes, please sign below and send to:
The Great Ape Project–International, PO Box 19492, Portland, OR 97280-0492, USA
or to your national section of the Great Ape Project

There is room for additional endorsements if your family or friends would like to sign (please print clearly).

Name:	Address:
Signature:	Email:

Name:	Address:
Signature:	Email:

Name:	Address:
Signature:	Email:

Name:	Address:
Signature:	Email:

Name:	Address:
Signature:	Email:

The Declaration on Great Apes can also be signed online at GAP's website: ***www.greatapeproject.org***

THE GREAT APE PROJECT, *edited by Paola Cavalievi and Peter Singer.*

Bridging the GAP: A DECLARATION ON GREAT APES.

THE PLIGHT OF THE OREGON MONKEYS
by Matt Rossell and Leslie Hemstreet

Abuse Exposed!

The Oregon Regional Primate Research Center (ORPRC) of the Oregon Health Sciences University (OHSU) has been taking a well-deserved beating in the Oregon and national media over the past year.

This was the result of two "whistle-blowers," one a primate technician and the other a US Department of Agriculture (USDA) Animal Welfare Act inspector, coming forward at an In Defense of Animals press conference in August 2000.

Painful evidence of animal cruelty includes video footage of ORPRC's electro-ejaculation procedure, in which technicians electrocute the penises of fully conscious male monkeys to obtain semen samples.

Other video, secretly taken by myself (Matt Rossell), depicts monkeys driven mad by isolation and maternal deprivation, attacking their own bodies and inflicting serious injuries.

More than a dozen abnormal behaviors result from housing monkeys alone in cages little more than two by two feet (0.6 by 0.6 meters) for their entire lives.

Bored and lonely, many monkeys in labs pull their hair out, smear and eat their own feces, and circle and pace neurotically awaiting the next experimental procedure.

For more details about the Oregon Regional Primate Center, please check this web site:

http://www.vivisectioninfo.org/ohsu/

USDA in Collusion

Dr. Isis Johnson Brown, Oregon's former USDA inspector, quit in frustration because her superiors refused to support her efforts to uphold the Animal Welfare Act.

She stated:

The USDA inspection system is comprised of a "good old boy" network that blatantly defies federal laws which, even if they were enforced, are too ineffectual to protect the animals. More than once, I was instructed by a supervisor to make a personal list of violations of the law, cut that list in half, and then cut that list in half again before writing up my inspection reports. My willingness to uphold the law during my site visits at the Primate Center led to me being "re-trained" several times by higher-ups in the USDA. I recognize the system is not set up to protect the animals but instead the financial interests of the research labs.

Criticism From Within

ORPRC administers inhumane care by any standards, including those of primate researcher Carol Shively, who was hired by the OHSU to review their programs at ORPRC. Shively called electro-ejaculation "inhumane" and criticized the lack of social housing—more than 1,200 monkeys are housed alone.

Dr. Shively stated,

The consensus of the scientific community is that these monkeys are dependent upon their social relationships for their physical and psychological well-being.

Shively also stated that depriving primates of social housing causes pathological behavior such as pacing, self-aggression, and hair-plucking to the

This infant is one of many deprived of their mother's love and kept isolated in small cages

IPPL NEWS ——— August 2001

3

IPPL News: AUGUST 2001 (p.3).

point of nudity.

That's what happens to animals that have evolved to be social when they are singly housed. It's entirely preventable.

"Model Institution"

So what does the Oregon Primate Center have to say in its defense? OHSU Provost Leslie Hallick calls their Primate Center a "model" for the industry. If Oregon is a "model," what does that say for the other seven Regional Primate Research Centers—and all the other primate labs?

Perhaps it tells us that the Oregon Primate Center demonstrates the standard neglect and inhumane treatment found nationwide?

Capuchins Freed!

Through local campaigns and as a result of the criticism of the local media, we were able to free 22 capuchin monkeys. They were released to zoos where they are now breathing fresh air, getting produce, feeling the sun and, best of all, living together in groups for the first time in more than 20 years.

We wish we could produce the same "happy ending" for all the ORPRC monkeys.

CALL TO ACTION

Through coordinated grassroots action and a coalition of national and international advocacy groups, we can look forward to the day when these horrific experiments are put to a stop and when all of the animals are retired to sanctuaries. Here is what you can do to help the thousands of monkeys living at the eight U.S. federally-funded primate centers.

Readers living in the United States, please get out your pens and write your representative and senators. To locate these officials, check www.congress.org and enter your zip code; the right names will appear on your monitor. Express your concern over the fate of U.S. laboratory primates. Request a congressional investigation into the ethical practices of all the centers. Ask that a congressional oversight committee investigate the weak enforcement of the US Animal Welfare Act, especially the extremely serious allegation by Dr. Isis Johnson Brown that she was repeatedly asked to ignore violations of the Act and to rewrite her inspection reports, deleting most of the violations.

Note that the whole world is becoming aware of the waste of taxpayer dollars and of the suffering of the wonderful animals at the Oregon Primate Center and other laboratories. Let them know that you think the public deserves access to all information about what is going on inside Oregon's publicly funded Primate Center, and comment that additional oversight is necessary to improve conditions internally and eliminate what we believe to be redundant and often ludicrous research.

(Name of your representative)
House of Representatives
Washington DC 20515, USA

(Names of your senators)
Senate Office Building
Washington DC 20510, USA

Readers living outside the United States should communicate their concern to the US Ambassador in the US Embassy in the capital city of their country of residence.

If you would like to start a similar campaign in your area or want to use information and images from this campaign, please contact Matt Rossell or Leslie Hemstreet at primates@aracnet.com

---

LETTERS WORK BETTER THAN E-MAIL!

If you want to make sure your US congressional representatives learn of your opinion on any issue, try to avoid using e-mail. Traditional letters and faxes are more effective.

According to an 18 March article carried by the Reuters news service, members of the US Congress are **"inundated with so many e-mail messages from constituents and special interest groups—80 million alone last year—that lawmakers routinely ignore most of them."**

The Congress On-line project noted that, besides constituent mail, lawmakers receive endless lobbying messages from advocacy groups and corporations. These are not necessarily from constituents. In some cases the deluge of e-mail is so heavy that mail delivery can be delayed for several days!

IPPL suggests that there is nothing better then sending old-fashioned personal letters to your own representative or senator. Be sure to concentrate your letter on one important issue as different staff members handle each issue. Be careful not to write too often as you don't want to be written off as a "pen pal."

Page copied from IPPL News *(courtesy of G.M.).*
Permission to use granted by Dr. Shirley McGreal,
founder and chairwoman of IPPL.

IPPL News: August 2001 (p.4).

Chapter 13. The United States/South American Connection

(Caliente Racetrack in Mexico; dog racing in other countries)

In November 1992, Jorge Hank, owner of the Caliente Racetrack in Tijuana, Mexico, admitted in a televised interview (Channel 10, in San Diego) that he killed racers who stopped winning and fed them to his large cat collection. (*Source:* The Animal Press, San Diego, CA, November 1992.) The track, which has since closed, was an end of the line track for many American racers who had stopped winning, and was known for horrendous cruelty.

Dog racing is active in England, Scotland, Wales, Ireland, Spain, Italy, Sweden, Australia, New Zealand, Macau, Mexico, Guam (a territory of the U.S.), Abu Dubai (a city in war-torn Bosnia) and the Philippines. It recently was introduced in Vietnam, Korea and China. Be aware that dog flesh is eaten in the latter four countries.

Vietnam

Dog racing started in Vietnam in 1999, as a joint venture between the government of Vietnam and a British Virgin Islands corporation. The racers are trained in Ireland. (*Source:* GNN, Fall 1999.)

Macau

Macau is a tiny Portuguese overseas territory not far from Hong Kong. Greyhound racing has been active in Macau since 1963. An English trainer who spent more than a year there reported that, "the dogs were literally raced to death and rarely lasted 6 months. The cruelty is unbelievable." (*Source:* GNN, Fall 1998. GNN's source was the Hong Kong Standard, Harold Bruning.)

Spain

The following was written by Louise Coleman in the December 1997, issue of The Home Stretch, newsletter of Greyhound Friends, (p. 5). Permission to reprint granted by Louise Coleman.

On October 19, Marion Fitzgibbon, President of the Irish SPCA, left for a five-day visit to Spain with an Irish veterinarian, the CEO of the Irish SPCA and the Chief Inspector of the RSPCA in England to assess the conditions for greyhounds at the two tracks in Barcelona and the one in Palma de Mallorca. The manager of the Palma track asked the group to leave because he could not guarantee their safety. Marion wanted to register a complaint with the veterinarian at the track just so there would be a record of their inquiry. No such person was available. The following is a brief report she wrote in the middle of the night when she couldn't sleep after what she saw:

"The visit to Barcelona and Palma was more traumatic than I could ever have imagined. The overall feeling I experienced was one of shattering sadness for the greyhounds and an overpowering sense of shame that I am Irish. The immensity of the problem and the endless numbers of Irish greyhounds in an abject state of misery was overwhelming.

"Where can we start? What can we do? I have asked myself over and over again during the last five days.

"Details of the use and abuse of these beautiful animals will be contained in the veterinary reports.

"My abiding memory will be one of seeing dogs that could hardly walk being led up to race at the Palma track. If there is such a place as hell, then surely I have been there and that place is called Palma de Race Track!"

– *Marion Fitzgibbon*

(End of the Home Stretch excerpt.)

Strange Fruit

The song "Strange Fruit," music and lyrics written by Lewis Allan in 1939, was sung by Billy Holiday in the 1972 Paramount film "Lady Sings the Blues." It describes the horror and brutality of lynching, the lynching of innocent and powerless black persons in the U.S., especially in the South. To be lynched is to be hanged, burned or otherwise killed by a mob without legal authority. Wherever lynching is common practice, so is the term lynch law, which in fact encourages murder by a mob.

Out for a night of fun, it was common practice for local rednecks and others to fill their bellies with whiskey, then find themselves a black man, and string him up. More often than not, local law enforcement persons participated in the murder or turned the other way, and untold numbers of black persons were hanged, burned to death or both.

Out of a sense of rage and sadness, a man named Lewis Allan wrote a poem which he set to music and called "Strange Fruit." It is a poem/song with a powerful message that describes southern trees which bear a strange fruit. What is this strange fruit? It is black bodies, their eyes bulging and their mouths twisted, swinging in the southern breeze and hanging from southern poplar trees.[3] Are lynchings things of the past or do they continue to the present? To find out, contact: The Southern Poverty Law Center, 400 Washington Avenue, Montgomery AL 36104. The SPLC is a non-profit organization that fights racial hate and hate crimes via education and litigation.

Now let us proceed to dog racing in Spain.

Scooby in Spain

Scooby is an organization dedicated to protecting animals of other species. It has a small refuge located in Medina del Campo, Spain, which its founder describes as a small town of 20,000 persons and a town with many problems. Señor Fermín Perez Martín, a school teacher and Scooby's founder and president, is constantly receiving calls from persons in different parts of Spain asking him to take in Greyhounds who are at serious risk. Between March 1998 and March 1999, Scooby rescued several hundred Greyhounds, 175 of them in the latter year alone. He writes that bull fighting and Greyhound cruelty are two of the worst animal welfare problems in Spain. This is especially true of the galgos.

Galgos are Spanish Greyhounds who are bred on farms in rural areas for hunting purposes. The exact number bred isn't known, but it reportedly is enormous. According to Señor Martín, six or seven females must be bred in order to obtain one "good" dog, meaning a dog hunters consider suitable for hunting. The others are disposed of. Brutally. In addition, Señor Martín writes that the dogs are poorly fed, lack veterinary care, and large numbers arrive at Scooby sick, diseased, and filled with parasites and ticks.

Young galgos are first trained by being walked. As they pick up speed, they're tied to a motor vehicle and forced to run. If they don't run fast enough or stumble, they're killed. Brutally. Usually by hanging. Training usually is completed by the start of each hunting season and the killing continues. Señor Martín explains that galgos are quite intelligent and sometimes they decide not to follow a hare as they were taught to do. Instead, they take a short cut to capture the little animal. But when they do this they are disqualified as "dirty" and "worthless." Their punishment: Death by hanging.

Other galgos are disqualified as "dirty" and "worthless" when they lose interest in chasing hares. This probably happens because the hares are taken away from them, meaning they're denied the rewards of the hunt. Most galgos survive just one hunting season before they're hanged. None survive more than three seasons before being hanged, impaled or burned to death. Why such unspeakable cruelty? Who knows? Perhaps the more accustomed people become to a particular form of cruelty, the more they accept it as a way of life, a tradition. In addition, the mentality behind it is that it's cheaper to breed new galgos for each hunting season instead of feeding and sheltering the others for nine months until the start of the next hunting season.

When the hunting season ended in January 1999, Scooby took in 220 galgos. But there was room for only seventy-five, so Anne Finch (Greyhounds in Need in Great Britain) and other good persons took them as fast as they could so that Scooby would be able to rescue more doomed galgos. Hunters constantly threaten Señor Martín that they'll hang the dogs if he doesn't take them. These threats continue to the present.

The demand for galgos is so great during the peak of each hunting season that many are stolen. In just one year (1998), 1,000 were reported stolen. The number is thought to be much higher because few hunters report the thefts, believing it won't do any good. Between July 1998, and July 1999, the Scooby refuge was broken into and twenty-five galgos were stolen, galgos who previously had been discarded as "dirty" and "worthless." It's not known if they were sent to other parts of Spain or to Portugal, or to Arab countries. Try to imagine the fate that awaited and continues to await them there.

When Scooby first opened its doors in 1997, it rescued three galgos. The following year, after it reported and publicized the hangings, it rescued 300 galgos. The end-of-year total was expected to be about 600. The present refuge is a small warehouse that is inadequate and unsuitable for dogs or any living creatures. Scooby has acquired some land on which to build a new refuge, but lacks the funds. It needs financial help worldwide. The situation is quite desperate because, as already noted, Señor Martín constantly receives calls from persons who want to "dispose" of their galgos; they threaten to brutally murder them if he doesn't make room for them.

The mass hangings in Spain continue. In January 2000, animal activists in Spain found the bodies of dead dogs in a field near the town of Avalo, population about 7,000. Some were galgos and some were retired racers who originated in Great Britain and Ireland. Local people say the hangings go back to medieval times, when feudal lords hanged "worthless" Greyhounds as a warning to peasants to behave. (*Source:* GNN, Spring 2000, p. 6.)

NOTE: *Hanging galgos is a very old Spanish tradition. So is bull-fighting/murder. But being a tradition, no matter how old the tradition is, doesn't make it right. Some traditions are heinous and should be criminalized and forever banned.*

Ireland

Dog racing is very popular in Ireland, where about 14,000 Greyhounds reportedly are bred each year (some say this number is too low), of whom about 1,000 are exported to Spain for racing purposes.

Incidentally, the fate that awaits retired racers in Spain isn't much kinder than the galgos' fate. Although the vast majority of Irish Greyhounds are exported to Great Britain, many are sent to Italy and other countries. Marion Fitzgibbons, president of the Irish SPCA, is trying to stop the sale of Irish Greyhounds to Spain, and the Royal SPCA also has called for a halt to these sales. But exports and sales continue.

It's been reported that retired racers in Ireland often are abandoned and sometimes drowned. Few are adopted because the dog racing industry in Ireland has convinced the public that racers are strictly economic commodities who do not make good companion animals. The lucky ones are rescued by Greyhounds in Need and other compassionate persons and groups. Louise Coleman of Greyhound Friends has brought some Irish racers to the United States and placed them in adoptive homes.

Great Britain

It's been reported that each year in Great Britain many thousands of Greyhounds are bred for racing purposes, some of whom are exported to other countries. It's also been reported that at the end of their racing careers some racers are thrown into the sea with weights around their necks, while others are "battered" to death. (*Source:* GNN, Spring 2000.)

In February 2000, the mutilated body of a former British racer was found in a plastic bag along a highway. He was about three years old, had a fractured skull, a broken neck, and one ear had been cut off to prevent his *owner* from being identified. (*Source:* GNN, Spring 2000.)

In February 2001, twelve racers died at a dog track in Birmingham, England, after eating their dinner. Contaminated meat was the suspected cause. After a forensic analysis of both the meat and the dead dogs, it was determined that they had died from eating meat that was contaminated with local anesthetics and barbiturates. These drugs are commonly used to euthanize horses.

An official of one British racing group suggested that racers be fed meat that is fit for human consumption, but an official from another group disagreed. He said, "The problem is with horsemeat – horses are often kept as pets and people prefer to use drugs rather than shoot them." It is suspected that forty-seven racers who died of food poisoning in 1998, had been fed the same kind of contaminated meat, which is known as a drug cocktail. (*Source:* GNN, Spring 2001, p. 6.)

Track Closings Worldwide

As already noted, in the United States seven dog tracks have closed since 1991.

In early 1999, a dog track in Mallorca, Spain, closed and several hundred dogs were rescued by Scooby and Greyhounds in Need. Soon thereafter, the Barcelona track closed and another few hundred dogs were at serious risk. It appeared that the dogs would be put to death but, after an international out-cry, the order of execution was cancelled and Scooby and Greyhounds in Need found temporary homes for them.

In June 1999, the dog track in Naples, Italy, closed with 300 Irish-bred Greyhounds desperately needing rescuing. Homes were found for many of them in England, France, Belgium, Holland, Germany, Switzerland, Austria and Luxembourg. A few came to the United States.

There's been rumor that a track in Rome was to close with 500 racers at risk and more closings may be expected. If Scooby and Greyhounds in Need are to save these former racers from a horrible death, they will need financial help from good people everywhere.

Greyhounds in Need may be reached at: Greyhounds in Need, 5 Greenway, Egham Surrey TW20 9PA, England; or P.O. Box 460, Hagaman NY 12086.

Track Openings Worldwide — Bad News for Greyhounds

Nuevo Laredo Downs, a dog track in Mexico that closed in 1988, is expected to reopen in 2003. It was purchased by an enterprise in North Dakota. (*Source:* GNN, Winter 2001-2002.)

It appears that dog racing will start once again in Russia, where it had been active until the Bolshvik Revolution in 1917. The Bolsheviks banned it not because it was brutal and cruel, but because they considered it a form of bourgeois entertainment. (*Source:* GNN, Winter 2001-2002.)

Top: Pili from Cordoba, taking a nap in Perrotel boarding kennels, Alicante, Spain. She is now in Belgium.

Center: Khalif, a longhaired galgo from Medina del Campo, Spain, on a beanbag in Belgium.

Photos courtesy of Anne Finch, GREYHOUNDS IN NEED.

Bottom: Scotti from Granada, having a stretch in Perrotel boarding kennels, Alicante, Spain. He is now in France.

INTERNATIONAL NEWS UPDATE

Horror in Spain: Barbaric Killing of Greyhounds Exposed

[This story is brutally graphic. Reader discretion is strongly advised. - Ed.]

Medina del Campo: A four-page investigative report recently published in the Spanish magazine *Interviu* confirms earlier accounts of the barbaric custom of hanging greyhounds at the end of their usefulness, either as racers or as coursing and hunting dogs.

"The greyhound who runs well dies by hanging so he will have a quick death in thanks for his service," is a common refrain among greyhound owners. Greyhounds who don't perform well, however, suffer an agonizingly slow death: they are hung by the neck from tree limbs with their rear feet just touching the ground and die from asphyxiation when their legs tire and give out from under them. Others are hung by one leg or simply tied to a tree and left to die slowly from hunger and thirst.

Interviu reported that hundreds of greyhounds were found hanging from trees in the pine groves near this small town 100 miles northwest of Madrid in the Castile and Leon region of the country but added the practice is also common in Zamora, Andalucia and Madrid. Nearly a dozen full-color photographs by *Interviu* photojournalist Fernando Abizanda accompanied the text and provided uncompromisingly graphic evidence of this unspeakable inhumanity.

Several local greyhound owners vehemently denied any responsibility for the atrocities and told *Interviu* that outsiders were to blame. An unidentified person was quoted as saying, "When we kill our greyhounds we bury the animals . . . we have dogs who are 14 years old and they are here."

The barbaric Spanish practice of killing unwanted greyhounds by hanging was first exposed by Madrid-based Asociacion Nacional Para La Defensa De Los Animales (ANDA) last year. Photographs taken by ANDA were sent to the Brussels-based Eurogroup for Animal Welfare, who issued a press release several months ago calling for international support to stop the killings.
Source: *Interviu:* Loles Silva

What you can do: Please write to the following officials and respectfully request their help in stopping the export of Irish and English greyhounds to Spain.

The Honorable Sean O'Huiginn
Irish Ambassador to the United States
2334 Massachusetts Avenue NW
Washington D.C. 20008

The Honorable Richard N. Gardner
United States Ambassador to Spain
American Embassy
Madrid, Spain
APO, AE 09642 (32-cent postage)

Article copied from GREYHOUND NETWORK NEWS
(courtesy of G.M.).

International News Update: FALL 1997.

INTERNATIONAL NEWS UPDATE

Greyhound Rescuers Appeal for Halt to Torture of Irish Greyhounds in Spain

Belfast, Northern Ireland: Sunday People published an article July 29 headlined, "Hounded to Death by Fiends," which began as follows: "A once-proud Irish greyhound hangs from a tree after months of savage abuse at the hands of cruel Spanish masters. The battered five-year-old was kept in a cramped, sweltering hovel, pumped with drugs, forced to race, made to breed over and over again and then strung up and used for target practice." The article included a photograph of the hanging greyhound and an inset photo showing the bullet wound that ended the dog's torment.

According to *Sunday People*, the latest figures show there are now more than 800 Irish dogs in Barcelona alone. The malnourished dogs are crammed into meter-square cages and many are suffering from parasitic diseases.

Rena Maguire of Belfast, Northern Ireland, a volunteer for Greyhounds in Need (GIN), said the treatment of the dogs is nothing short of a European scandal. "The Irish Greyhound Board (IGB) has said it is against this, but it does nothing to educate owners here to tell them that this could happen to their dogs," she said.

GIN is a registered charity founded by Anne Finch of Surrey, England. The group has been responsible for rescuing hundreds of Irish greyhounds from the Spanish tracks and placing them in homes throughout Europe.

Paddy O'Dwyer of the IGB said he knew of the stories of mistreatment, but said that Spain was not under the IGB'S jurisdiction. "We can't be charged with responsibility for what happens in Spain," he said. "Spain is a minute market with the bulk of retired dogs going to Britain."

"There are thousands of Spanish hunting clubs and they're not monitored by law in any way," Maguire said. "At the end of each season the dogs are taken out, shot, beaten, hanged, burned or impaled," she said. Witnesses have said that many huntsmen take "great pleasure" in seeing the dogs writhe in agony before they die.

"It is heartbreaking to think how people can send these dogs to a life of misery," Maguire said. "Education is so important because if more people were to know the truth then hopefully they might begin to boycott the Spanish market."

"We are bringing as many dogs back as we can and they stay at the shelter in Bournemouth," Maguire said. "We've gathered boxes of soft bedding and food for the dogs and now we just need to get it over there," she said. *Sunday People* appealed to its readers for help in transporting the supplies from Ireland to England.
Source: (London) *Sunday People*: Jason Johnson

Article copied from
GREYHOUND NETWORK NEWS
(courtesy of G.M.).

International News Update:
FALL 2001.

INTERNATIONAL NEWS UPDATE

"The Sprinter Slave Trade"
Second-Rate Irish Hounds Sold to Spanish Agents

Cork, Ireland: In September 1997 *Der Speigel* reporter Renate Nimtz-Koster attended trial runs for the fall greyhound auctions held at the Cork racetrack. Her article for the internationally known German magazine painted a sickening portrait of Irish breeders, whose brutality is comparable to their Spanish counterparts.

At the end of one race a dog named Tawnies Delight embarrassed her owner in front of the crowd by running across the arena eluding capture. "She's no good," the spectators shouted. Later in the day at a local pub, one breeder was overheard to say, "If that runaway were mine, I would make her die a slow death. That bitch does not deserve a quick death at all."

Fortunately for Tawnies Delight, Marion Fitzgibbon, President of the ISPCA (Irish Society for the Prevention of Cruelty to Animals), was at the auction that day and bought the 2-year-old greyhound for £100. "Sooner or later they will all be losers," Fitzgibbon said. "Greyhounds that fail forfeit their lives."

Almost daily, Fitzgibbon and her assistants rescue emaciated greyhounds throughout the countryside. Many owners consider it cheaper and easier to drown the dogs in canals or leave them tied up in remote locations to die of starvation. According to Fitzgibbon, about 5,000 Irish greyhounds a year meet this fate. "A quick and easy death by injection would be a stroke of luck for the poor animals," she said.

An even worse fate awaits Ireland's second-rate greyhounds. They are sold at auction to Spanish wholesale buyers for as little as £25. After a long transport in narrow cages, the dogs are crammed into deplorable mass kennels at the Spanish tracks in Barcelona and Mallorca. After a brief racing career, the dogs are either impaled or hung on trees to die an agonizingly slow death, as reported in the Spanish magazine *Interviu* last year. This occurs primarily in the area around Medina del Campo, a town in the Valladolid region of Spain. *[See GNN Fall 1997 and Spring 1998.]*

The increasing number of Irish greyhounds exported to Spain is a direct result of a 1994 EU (European Union) agricultural sub-directive to increase the number of dogs bred in order to expand the export market to countries other than England, the U.S. and Spain. Sweden recently became a new market and Irish dogs may be racing in Pakistan in the future.

The EU, which dates back to 1951, was formed by treaty alliances between the democratic states of Europe. The EU aims to promote unrestricted trade and political union among its 15 member states. Spain became a member in 1986; Sweden joined the EU in 1995.

Medina del Campo Update

Local resident and animal welfare advocate Fermin Perez Martin, who documented the hanging of greyhounds last year, reported recently that ten abandoned greyhounds a week were rescued when hunting season ended in the spring. A temporary refuge has been set up in a rented warehouse in Medina to house the greyhounds.

Anne Finch, founder of Greyhounds In Need, has made seven trips to Medina this year, each time bringing urgently needed supplies for the dogs. On each return journey, at least six greyhounds are brought to safety in Belgium, France and Switzerland.

Perez and Finch are working to establish a permanent sanctuary in Medina. Jose Valin, Regional Agricultural Minister, has promised to provide funds for the building's construction. Medina's mayor, however, is reluctant to issue the building permit. *GNN* readers who want to help can write to Anne Finch at: 5 Greenways, Egham, Surrey, TW 20 9PA, England.

Sources: *Der Speigel:* Renate Nimtz-Koster
Greyhounds In Need Newsletter

Information Packet Available

Vermont-based Save the Greyhound Dogs! has prepared an information packet on Spain that includes news articles, photos, sample letters to embassies (names and addresses included), airlines, importers and exporters of Spanish goods. For a copy, send $5 to STGD!, P.O. Box 8981, Essex, VT 05451.

Article copied from
GREYHOUND NETWORK NEWS
(courtesy of G.M.)

International News Update:
FALL 1998.

INTERNATIONAL NEWS UPDATE

Sudden Closure of Barcelona Racetrack Imperils 250 Irish Greyhounds

Spain: Canodromo Pabellon, one of two greyhound tracks in Barcelona, closed suddenly at the end of February, leaving 250 Irish greyhounds, mostly bitches, at great risk. Mass euthanasia of the dogs, scheduled to begin March 17, was halted at the eleventh hour after an international protest by Anne Finch of Greyhounds in Need, Surrey, England, Louise Coleman of Greyhound Friends, Massachusetts, USA, and local Barcelona veterinarian Albert Sorde and his wife Anna Clements.

Barcelona Vice Mayor Pilar Rahola canceled the euthanasia order. She then contacted Beatriz Cayuela, head of the Animal Protection Society, which operates a shelter 35 miles north of Barcelona in Vic, who agreed to give the dogs temporary shelter. Rahola also convinced the city council to provide funds to feed the dogs.

Coleman, accompanied by photo journalist John Mottern, arrived in Barcelona March 18 for a week's stay. Randy Barrow, director of Greyhound Friends of North Carolina, and Ralph Yerex, DVM, arrived a few days later with medical supplies. Yerex and Sorde provided some medical care for the dogs but more is needed.

Mottern's photographs of the dogs and the primitive conditions at the refuge were e-mailed to European and U.S. wire services. The ensuing news reports brought attention to the dogs' plight and helped generate donations for Greyhounds in Need. In late March the Irish SPCA assumed responsibility for the dogs and will attempt to filter them into homes in Europe.

Former ISPCA president Marion Webb arrived at the shelter March 24 and plans an indefinite stay to monitor the dogs. Regrettably, Webb was unable to prevent Cayuela from adopting out 104 of the dogs locally. According to Coleman, 50 were placed with upscale Barcelona families, but the others were unwittingly placed with questionable owners; 110 dogs remain on site.

Just before the Barcelona crisis unfolded, the Balear track on the island of Mallorca closed. A British vet who visited all the Spanish tracks in November said conditions at Balear were "hideous." Finch said the owners run the dogs into the ground. "One of the dogs we rescued had four broken legs. The vet said it must have been run on three broken legs and then broken the fourth under the strain," she said.

Neither the Pabellon track in Barcelona nor the Balear track on Mallorca is expected to reopen. The second Barcelona

Photo by John Mottern

Louise Coleman checks on four greyhounds in a holding kennel at the shelter in Vic, Spain.

track, Meridiana, remains open but its future, and the future of the 800 greyhounds kenneled there, is questionable.

Meanwhile, the greyhound refuge Finch helped to establish in Medina del Campo, run by Fermin Perez of Protectora de Animales, is bursting with 300 greyhounds; the unheated warehouse building holds 75. Perez reported in January that the hangings have decreased; some hunters are leaving their dogs at the door of the refuge.

The number of greyhounds displaced in Spain has reached enormous proportions. Anne Finch is the dogs' best hope but her funds are running out. *GNN* readers who wish to help may send a donation to: 5 Greenways, Egham, Surrey TW20 9PA, England.

Sources: *The (London) Mirror:* Jeremy Armstrong
Associated Press Worldstream Wire

Article copied from **GREYHOUND NETWORK NEWS** *(courtesy of G.M.).*

International News Update: SPRING 1999.

INTERNATIONAL NEWS UPDATE

Racetracks to Spread Throughout Vietnam and into Cambodia

[**Editor's Note**: *The following information was excerpted from the transcript of a presentation made by Nguyen Ngoc My at the international conference of the World Greyhound Racing Federation held in Sydney, Australia, in November 2000.*

Nguyen is the general manager of Sports and Entertainment Services (SES), the company operating the Ba Ria Vung Tau racetrack. Nguyen, who is also the chairman of Indo China Racing and Entertainment, has been granted a 30-year license for the development of greyhound racing in Cambodia. A racing facility has already been identified in Phomn Phenn.

The transcript was given to Louise Coleman, director of Greyhound Friends, Inc., Hopkinton, Mass., while she was in Dublin attending the International Greyhound Welfare Forum in February. The semi-annual meetings are chaired by the London-based National Canine Defence League.]

■ Greyhound racing commenced May 5, 2000 with an eight-race program. All races were eight dog fields over 450 meters (M). Race meetings were held once a week until mid-July when one distance race of 630 M per week was added. Beginning in mid-August, flying races of 260 M were introduced [no definition given] in conjunction with adding a second race meeting per week.

■ The track is a tight two-turn circuit of 393 M. Dogs race in three distances: 260 M, 450 M, and 630 M.

■ Betting turnover increased exponentially during the formative period. In less than eight weeks betting turnover grew by more than 100 percent. Average attendance at Saturday race meetings is 3,500 to 4,000.

■ There are six kennel blocks, each holding 38 greyhounds; three isolation blocks contain eight kennels used for quarantine purposes, and for sick and/or injured dogs.

■ SES has begun a breeding program to supplement the need to import racing greyhounds. The program is expected to be fully effective within two years.

■ Public ownership of greyhounds will be introduced in 2001. The greyhounds will be kept at Ba Ria and trained by SES trainers. The owners will pay a monthly training fee and receive prize money.

■ SES plans to develop six more dog tracks throughout Vietnam. Other planned locations are Ho Chi Minh City, Hanoi, Hai Phong, Da Nang, Nha Trang, and Can Tho.

In his conclusion, Nguyen said, " I am pleased to report that the local Vietnamese have embraced greyhound racing with similar passion to that of other countries which host the sport. It is therefore timely to move on and continue to develop a network of greyhound tracks throughout Vietnam."

For continued updates on the developing Vietnam situation, visit http://www.ameurogreyhoundalliance.org

Article copied from GREYHOUND NETWORK NEWS
(courtesy of G.M.).

International News Update: SUMMER 2001.

INTERNATIONAL NEWS UPDATE

AUSTRALIA

Glenelg, New South Wales: Una Jones, a greyhound trainer for the past 30 years, was disqualified from holding a training license for two years after the local racing authority found her guilty of administering drugs to greyhounds and giving false evidence to the stewards. Jones, originally from Broken Hill, was also barred from thoroughbred, harness, and greyhound tracks for the same period.

Jones, 76, told *The Advertiser* Oct. 9, "I just can't stop crying. Training them and racing them is my life and now it's gone. I'm too old to go through this. They aren't just animals or a job, they're my family."

The racing authority began its inquiry after Jones pleaded guilty in District Court June 26 to growing four kilograms of cannabis and possessing the drug for supply. Jones admitted to the court that she had been told the secret to success in greyhound racing was to feed her dogs cannabis. She said she had been given nine seeds and planted them. The plants grew almost to the ceiling of her flat before they were discovered.

Jones was given a six-month suspended sentence by the District Court and placed on a $1,000 good behavior bond for 18 months.

Source: *The Advertiser*: Danielle Gordon

Townsville, Northern Territory: Brenda Burns, owner of one of Townsville's largest kennels, turned in her license in disgust after stewards ruled against her husband Noel Burns Oct. 9. Burns, a handler for his wife's greyhounds, told the press the following day that he had taken three of their dogs to a veterinarian and had them put down. He added that most of the 40 dogs in their kennel, including 20 puppies, would likely meet the same fate.

"Why hang on to them, I'm not going to feed them for nothing," he said. "I don't like doing it, you whelp them and rear them, but what do you do? You can't give them away. Nobody wants them," Burns said. "I'm a bit over 60 years old and on the dole, so if the dogs don't pay I can't afford to keep them," he said.

Kate Miles, President of the Townsville Breeders Association, said good homes could be found for most of the dogs. "Maybe not all of them but a fair majority of them," she said. "I'm sure if the Burnses asked, people would be only too willing to try and help them out."

Noel Burns was disqualified for 12 months and fined $500 after a steward's inquiry found him guilty of assaulting the chief steward. Burns, who reportedly threw a dog's registration papers at the steward, described the incident as "trivial."

Source: *Townsville Bulletin*: Craig Baxter

EUROPE

Armadale, Scotland: John Hefferman, owner of the Armadale Greyhound Track in West Lothian, announced earlier this year that the family-run track would close by the end of the year. Hefferman said, "We are looking for a builder to develop the track site into flats."

On Sept. 1, the nearby Wishaw greyhound track closed its doors, ending 70 years of dog racing. The impending closure of both tracks was reported in the Scottish media in early August, prompting animal welfare groups to issue a warning that the track closures will render hundreds of racing dogs worthless, leaving many to face a violent death [see *GNN* Summer 2001].

Sources: (Edinburgh) *Evening News*: Angie Brown
Scottish Daily Record

Wallyford, Scotland: Howard Wallace, an Edinburgh businessman, has filed a planning application at the East Lothian Council headquarters for a new greyhound track to be built on a wasteland in Wallyford at a cost of £8.4 million. Wallace said he hoped to have the stadium, to be called Victory Lane, opened by April or May 2002.

The stadium will feature an eight-lane, 500-meter track based on the Albion Park Greyhound Track in Brisbane, Australia, with an underground track heating system to allow winter racing. The four-story grandstand will include a restaurant with seating for 200, conference and lounge facilities, a promenade level for 300 spectators, and a ground-floor area for betting. The kennels will house 120 greyhounds.

Wallace said he is confident that the new stadium will attract patrons not only from throughout the central belt of Scotland, but from England and Ireland as well.

Source: *Scotland on Sunday*: Marti Hannan

Moscow, Russia: Thirteen teams of greyhound owners and more than one hundred of their dogs converged on the town of Novonikolayevsky in southern Russia Oct. 29 to begin two weeks of amateur racing and hare hunting in an event billed as the "Greyhound Games."

Judges determined the winners of various events based on speed and the condition of the hare's pelt when it is brought back. Novonikolayevsky, located in the Volgograd region, was chosen as the site of the games because of the abundance of hares in the area.

Russia had a long-standing tradition of greyhound racing and coursing that lasted until the 1917 revolution. After the Bolshevik's came to power, greyhound racing died out because it was regarded as a bourgeois pastime.

The sport has made a "timid" comeback since the fall of the Soviet Union, according to Marina Mansurova, a member of the Russian Association of Greyhound Racing Fans, organizer of the event. The association is hopeful that once the economy develops, greater numbers will be drawn to dog racing as a cheaper form of entertainment than horse racing.

Mansurova said there are greyhound-breeding centers in Moscow, Murmansk in the far north above the Arctic Circle, and Chelyabinsk in the Urals.

Sources: Agence France Presse
ITAR-TASS News Agency

NORTH AMERICA

Nuevo Laredo, Mexico: Nuevo Laredo Downs, closed since 1988, is expected to reopen for greyhound racing in 2003. Sergio Luis Cano, former general manager of the dog track, will manage the reopened track.

Cano, who currently runs a bar and betting club in Nuevo Laredo, said that Racing Services Inc. in Fargo, North Dakota, bought the track in October from a Veracruz racing family for a fraction of its original value. The track was built in 1983 at a cost of $19 million.

Cano, who plans to develop hotels in the area surrounding the track, said he believes the track has a better chance during its second run with the help of modern embellishments such as simulcasting.

Source: *Fort Worth Star-Telegram*: Karen Brooks

Article copied from
GREYHOUND NETWORK NEWS
(courtesy of G.M.)

International News Update: WINTER 2001-02.

Chapter 14. Death by Electrocution

The electrocutions took place at the Coeur d'Alene Greyhound Park in Post Falls, ID. (*Source:* The Spokesman-Review, staff writer J. Todd Foster, September 17, 1995.)

Chapter 16. It's Safer To Be a Legislator Than a Racer
(dog racing banned in Vermont)

Gator is the Greyhound responsible for the bill that banned dog racing in Vermont. It was signed into law in April 1995. Gator succumbed to bone cancer on July 3, 1999. He was Scotti Devens' beloved companion. Ms. Devens is the founder of Save The Greyhound Dogs! in Essex, VT.

Since former racers appear to be especially vulnerable to bone and other forms of cancer, some people are beginning to wonder if the steroids they're routinely given and the contaminated meat that many are fed might be contributing factors.

Epilogue 2. Shayna

Shayna and former racers everywhere will live on in the three bills that Rep. Shaun Kelly filed, in spite of the fact that none of them made it out of committee. These wonderful dogs will also live on in the ballot initiative that brought this deadly issue to the voters of Massachusetts in November 2000, in spite of the fact that we lost the election by less than 2%.

Epilogue 3. Murphy
(the compassion and empathy of animals of other species)

The ability of other-specied animals to feel compassion and empathy for their own and other species has been well documented. Here are just three examples:

Chief, a lab/malamute mix, heard some pitiful cries and bolted in their direction in spite of the pleas of his human companion to stay, and in spite of the three to six feet of snow that covered the area. Chief searched for and rescued a snowboarder who was lost in a remote area of the Mammoth Mountains in California. He was awarded the North Shore Animal League's Lewyt Award for demonstrating extraordinary heroism or compassion. (*Source:* Animal People, January/February 2000, p. 23.)

B.J., a former long-term shelter dog, discovered that his human baby companion was suffocating in her crib and alerted her father. The child required hospitalization, but recovered. B.J. also won the North Shore Animal League's Lewyt Award. (*Source:* Animal People, October 1999, p. 23.)

In June 1996, the Press Trust of India reported that a pack of feral dogs in Calcutta stood guard all night over a baby who had been abandoned at a garbage dump. She was rescued the following day and the dogs followed her and her rescuer to the police station, where they waited until she was taken to Mother Theresa's orphanage. (*Source:* Animal People, July 1997, p. 23.)

Endnotes

About Chapter 11:

[1] In March 2001, Amnesty International released a report called Abuse of Women in Custody – Sexual Misconduct and Shackling of Pregnant Women in which it wrote, "In this report, we examined the laws, policies and practices regarding the mistreatment of women prisoners in every state, the District of Columbia and the U.S. Bureau of Prisons.

"Our report shows that only two states have laws that meet Amnesty's minimum standards for safeguarding the human rights of female prisoners. Even more incriminating, four states permit a female to be held criminally liable for engaging in sexual conduct with a prison official – and in Arizona this can happen even if the inmate is the victim of rape.

"Furthermore, eighteen states and DC allow women to be restrained during labor and/or delivery. In some cases, women's legs are unshackled just moments before delivery, and reshackled just moments after." *(Printed with AIUSA permission.)*

Human rights abuses are rampant worldwide. They happen in every country, more in some countries than in others, more blood-chilling in some than in others. Humans have the ability to create a variety of diabolical killling methods that are beyond understanding, and which they use on members of thier own and other species.

Amnesty International is a human rights organization dedicated to the protection of human rights in the U.S. and worldwide. It investigates torture, murder and other forms of brutality worldwide and is a passionate foe of the death penalty. Through its efforts, large numbers of prisoners of conscience worldwide have been released. Its U.S. office is located in New York City.

A long-time member of AI, the author is hoping it will raise its powerful voice against the anti-semitism that is spreading viciously and violently across the U.S. (including on college campuses) and world-wide (see Summer 2002 and other editions of Response, a publication of the Simon Wiesenthal Center in Los Angeles, CA). Likewise, against the persecution of Falun Dafa practitoners in China. Falun Dafa has its roots in an ancient Chinese cultivation practice for body, mind and spirit. It is based on the universal principles of truth, compassion and forebearance/tolerance. It is neither religious nor political in character. Nevertheless, Falun Dafa practitioners in China are being arrested and blood-chillingly tortured and executed by the Chinese government because it considers Falun Dafa a threat to the brutal totalitarian Chinese regime. For more information, see: *www.falundafa.org*.

About Chapter 12:

2 Chimpanzees are being threatened with extinction not just by the research industry, but also by the logging industry, the "exotic" pet trade industries, and by the "bush meat" trade. Chimpanzees, orangutans, gorillas, elephants, and other species are being poached and murdered. For what? For their flesh. In fact, in Indonesia, 10,000 square kilometers of orangutan habitat were to be cleared and planted with rice, making orangutans easy prey for poachers. Friends of Animals (FOA) in Darien, CT, has worked tirelessly to reduce the amount of poaching in African countries. The Fund for Animals in Silver Spring, MD, is doing likewise in Africa and Asia.

And every day in Africa, great apes and elephants are being murdered to satisfy the culinary tastes of diners; likewise monkeys, baboons, wild cats, antelopes and birds, all of whom are being served in restaurants throughout Europe. This creates many baby orphans, who become victims of the exotic pet trade industry. But the price may be greater than diners bargain for, since primate flesh has been linked to some deadly diseases in humans. In fact, it is believed that there is a connection between eating nonhuman primates and contracting the Aids virus that kills humans. If so, perhaps this is the primates' revenge.

Now that the consumption of cow and other farm animal flesh has also been linked to deadly diseases in humans (another indication of the animals' revenge?), the demand for horse flesh abroad, where it's considered a delicacy, has risen drastically. Consequently, more and more of these magnificent creatures are being slaughtered worldwide to meet this ominous demand.

Although it is not legal to butcher/slaughter horses for human consumption in the U.S., it is legal to slaughter them for "pet" food in the U.S. and for export to other countries. Few are aware that the world of horses is a dark and ugly place, a very dark and very ugly place. Few are aware that horses and other "livestock" and "food" animals are among the most brutally enslaved species on the planet. Each year in the United States, many billions (about nine) of farm animals are mercilessly slaughtered/butchered for human consumption. And according to FARM, the number murdered worldwide in 2001 was almost forty-eight billion. (*Source:* FARM Report, Winter/Spring 2002. Its source was the United Nations Food and Agriculture Organization. FARM Report is a publication of the Farm Animal Reform Movement in Bethesda, MD.)

According to the American Horse Defense Fund (AHDF) in Potomac, MD, the total number of horses slaughtered worldwide in 2000 was 4,290,250. It has also been reported that in 2001, nearly 57,000 horses were slaughtered in the U.S. for human consumption worldwide. (*Source:* USDA.) Many, many more were slaughtered in the early and mid-1990s. The decrease may be atrributed to the large numbers of horse slaughterhouses that have since closed in the U.S.

As for the BLM's (Bureau of Land Management, Department of the Interior) blood-chilling persecution of America's wild horses, in deference to the powerful ranching interests – that's another story from hell.

Equine Rescue in Bedford, NY, was responsible for Brown Beauty's Bill, a 2002 ballot initiative to ban the slaughter of Massachusetts horses for human consumption. The Massachusetts Attorney General's Office confirmed that it received complaints from some voters who said that when they wanted to sign Brown Beauty's petition, signature collectors gave them an entirely different petition to sign, one on behalf of another ballot question which they didn't support. Who knows how many unsuspecting persons signed the latter? Consequently, Brown Beauty's Bill will not appear on the ballot in November 2002. For more information contact: Equine Rescue, P.O. Box 700, Bedford NY 10506.

About Chapter 13:

[3] Lewis Allan is the pseudonym used by Abel Meeropol. He and his wife are the adoptive parents of Ethel and Julius Rosenberg's two children. Mr. and Mrs. Rosenberg were executed in 1953, after one of the most heinous and hysterical witch hunt trials of the 20th century.

PART
FOUR

The Abolition
Movement

The Abolition Movement

Summary of the Battle to Ban Dog Racing in Massachusetts

1. Via the Legislature:

It was Shayna's discovery in a cemetery and her near tragic end that motivated me in early 1992, to engage in protests at various New England tracks with my friend Erika Hartman, and to start tabling at a local mall in order to expose the truth about dog racing. Between May and September 1992, Erika and I quietly protested with our signs at Green Mountain Dog Track in Pownal, VT. At first we did this together three or four times a week. Then we decided to do it alone in order to cover the track five or six times a week. Being a seasonal track, it would close in September. As already noted, a cruelty investigation in 1992, forced it to close permanently.

One day I realized that protesting at New England tracks and tabling at a mall weren't enough. A bill would have to be filed and passed that would end dog racing in Massachusetts. With this in mind I collected almost 1,000 signatures on a petition asking Representative Shaun Kelly (Dalton, MA) to file such a bill. He and I met for the first time on December 30, 1993, at which time I presented him with the petition and a good deal of informative and pertinent material. He agreed to file such a bill, but because the deadline for filing for the 1994 legislative session had already passed, it would have to be filed the following year, during the first week of December 1994. But a year is a long time to wait, so I had attractive postcards printed. They were addressed to Representative Kelly and featured Shayna's picture and a message explaining why a bill to abolish was so necessary. They were distributed throughout Massachusetts and included, but weren't limited to Representative Kelly's constituents. People were asked to sign the post cards and mail them to him.

House Bill 899 was filed in early December 1994. It was the first bill ever filed to end dog racing and make it illegal in a state where it was still legal and active. Having had no prior experience with legislation, I asked a large, well-funded organization to take on this formidable task. When it refused, I asked another to do so. It too refused. I then asked a third and it refused. Each gave the same reason: it would be a waste of time, money and staff to try to ban dog racing in a state where it was active. It made more sense, they said, to try to keep it out of states where it never had been. They were quite adamant, so this formidable task was mine.

Soon after *HB 899's* public hearing before the Joint Committee on Government Regulations at the State House in Boston in March 1995, more postcards were printed. This time they were addressed to the two chair and two co-chair of the joint committee, and included a message that asked them to report the bill out of committee favorably so that the House and Senate might debate and vote on it. Like the previous post cards, they featured Shayna's picture. In addition, a letter writing campaign directed at the four legislators was initiated. As a result, by 1996, the joint committee had a file almost a foot thick with mail in favor of abolition. It nevertheless sent the bill to a study committee, where it languished and finally died in July 1996. The following month I met three very special persons. The four of us would eventually become Massachusetts Citizens Against Dog Racing. They are Libby Frattaroli, Steven Baer and Robin Norton.

In December 1996, Rep. Kelly filed a second bill, *HB 3434*. Its public hearing in Boston was in March 1997, and the following month Massachusetts Citizens Against Dog Racing was founded. This bill, like its predecessor, was sent to a study committee. After its demise in the summer of 1998, I mentioned to Rep. Kelly that I felt pretty certain that if this issue were brought before the voters of Massachusetts, dog racing would become a thing of the past. He listened carefully, his eyes lit up, and he said he thought a ballot initiative was the way to go. But we both understood the incredible time, money and energy – both physical and mental – it would require.

In December 1998, Rep. Kelly filed a third bill, *HB 1926*, and at its public hearing in the State House on March 16, 1999, the room was filled to capacity. On the previous day impressive looking posters had been placed in the MBTA subway cars in Boston. They featured Shayna saying: "Please Don't Go To The Dog Track" – and explaining why.

Those who testified included MaCADR volunteers, other Greyhound advocates, and students from the Everett High School in Everett, MA. Arlene Cavanaugh, MaCADR volunteer, had taught the students respect and compassion for racers, and arranged for their appearance at the State House. They spoke beautifully. In addition, Rep. Kelly spoke eloquently and told members of the joint committee that if they sent this bill to a study committee, as they did the two previous bills (sending a bill to a study committee is a quiet way of killing it), MaCADR and other Greyhound advocates were prepared to bring the issue before the voters. Rep. John Locke, one of the bill's co-sponsors, also spoke eloquently on its behalf.

The Berkshire Eagle Editorials

Editorial copied from THE BERKSHIRE EAGLE *with permission.*

FRIDAY, MARCH 19, 1999:

An editorial addressing the previous day's article on banning dog racing *(see next page)*.

Pass the dog racing ban

Filed repeatedly over the years, a bill to ban dog racing sponsored by state Representative Shaun P. Kelly is at last gaining steam in the Statehouse. That's exactly as it should be: Dog racing is a cruel sport which mistreats animals, and, with only two tracks left in the state, the jobs and revenues the industry generates are paltry. Support for the ban is growing among many legislators, and the death of state Representative William G. Reinstein, who for years fought for the track in his district, removes a major obstacle to passage. Politics is a game of seizing advantage, and with public and legislative opinion on its side, the dog racing ban should be brought to the floor and passed.

The Berkshire Eagle

Pittsfield, Massachusetts, Thursday, March 18, 1999

Dog racing ban gaining steam in Statehouse

By Julie Jette
Eagle Statehouse Bureau

BOSTON — The standard-issue uniform for Beacon Hill lobbyists is the conservative business suit. But on Tuesday, the Statehouse was stormed by petitioners in fur coats — and on four legs.

A bill to ban dog racing was one of an avalanche of gambling bills considered at a hearing of the Joint Committee on Government Regulations. Filed repeatedly over the years by state Rep. Shaun P. Kelly, R-Dalton, the proposal may at last be gaining ground.

Local interest in Lanesboro

Although Berkshire County has no dog track, Kelly was pulled onto the issue by Greta Marsh, a Lanesboro resident who has been active with Massachusetts Citizens Against Dog Racing for several years.

The proposed ban generated as much emotion and verbiage as a bill that would allow the development of three gambling casinos in the state. With track officials reportedly at a conference in Florida, nearly all who testified did so in favor of the ban.

Proponents of racing will get their chance to speak at the next Government Regulations Committee in a few weeks.

And while much of the testimony was provided by several dozen greyhound activists — many of whom brought their slender, pointy-nosed pets along — many

lawmakers voiced their opposition to dog racing as well.

"I think it's sickening and revolting what we do to these dogs," said state Rep. John A. Locke, R-Wellesley. "I urge at least your formal support so we can debate this."

"These are animals that suffer and live miserable lives," said state Sen. Susan Fargo, D-Lincoln.

Even state Sen. James P. Jajuga, D-Methuen, who is the chief sponsor of the casino bill, submitted testimony in favor of Kelly's bill.

Kelly and others strongly believe that if the bill gets to the floor, proponents of the ban will prevail.

"I believe if it were roll-called in the House, it would win. I believe if it were roll-called in the Senate, it would win, and if it were put before the voters of Massachusetts, it would win," he said at Tuesday's hearing.

Dog racing opponents' arguments are numerous, but they boil down to this: The industry breeds numerous dogs for profit, most of whom never even see a racetrack and all of whom meet their demise once they no longer turn a profit for their owners unless they're lucky enough to be adopted.

Massachusetts requires that dogs be euthanized via lethal injection, but activists insist that many are exported out of state and killed in cheaper, more brutal ways.

There are only two dog tracks left in the state, the Wonderland

track in Revere and the Raynham-Taunton Greyhound Park in southeastern Massachusetts.

Together, the two tracks directly employ about 500 people. But Kelly says that even state Rep. Edward G. Connolly, D-Everett, whose district is next door to Revere, has endorsed the bill.

"It's a very popular bill," Kelly said.

The bill may also have its best chance in years of passing because of the death of state Rep. William F. Reinstein, D-Revere, a Ways and Means Committee member who for years fought for the track in his district.

The jobs that the bill would eliminate are surely what has blocked its passage up to now, but it's unclear whether Raynham- and Revere-area legislators will be able to successfully fight the bill without Reinstein's help.

But Kelly acknowledged, "It does, in fact, decimate an industry."

Other states that have outlawed dog racing have generally done so after tracks have gone out of business of their own accord or before they've been opened.

Even track owners admit their revenues are declining, but they would like the state to allow them to install slot machines to prop up their profits.

Kelly said it appears unlikely that House Speaker Thomas M. Finneran, D-Boston, will try to keep the bill from coming to the floor. But in the end, it may not matter what the committee does with his bill.

Article copied from THE BERKSHIRE EAGLE *with permission.*

THURSDAY, MARCH 18, 1999:
An article about the proposed ban on
dog racing in Massachusetts (HB 1926).

SHAYNA

The Greyhound Behind the Legislation that Would End Dog Racing in Massachusetts

During the winter of 1991, a brindle and white racer was discovered in a cemetery in Massachusetts. She was wearing her racing muzzle and, according to the tattoo in one ear, she soon would be four years old. Since that's considered pretty old for a racer, she must have won a good deal of money for her trainer/ owner. When finally rescued by an animal control officer, this former racer was near death from the elements, starvation and dehydration.

After restoring her to health, the animal control officer brought her to Greyhound Friends in Hopkinton, Massachusetts. The day after she arrived, a woman adopted her and named her Shayna, which means pretty in Yiddish. And so began that woman's long and difficult battle to legislate dog racing out of Massachusetts.

For more information about legislation that would end dog racing in Massachusetts, contact Massachusetts Citizens Against Dog Racing at P.O. Box 882, Lanesboro, MA 01237 in Western MA, and P.O. Box 533, East Boston, MA 02128 in Eastern MA.

Flier by G.M.

One of many fliers used by MaCADR to help raise awareness of the three bills to ban dog racing in Massachusetts.

BUMPER STICKER
& PHOTOS

Bumper sticker coutesy of of G.M.

Distibuted throughout Massachusetts starting in 1994 to raise public
awareness of the three bills filed in December of '94, '96 and '98.

Photo by G.M.

Former racers and their advocates gathered across the street from the
State House just prior to the public hearing of *House Bill 1926.* (March 1999)

2. Via The Ballot

A couple of months later, in May 1999, some of us felt pretty certain that *HB 1926* also would die. We felt that the joint committee had made its decision prior to the bill's public hearing (as well as prior to the two previous public hearings). It was clear that dog racing wouldn't be abolished via the legislature. Our only other option was the ballot. So MaCADR and other Greyhound advocates joined forces and formed a coalition whose mission was to ban dog racing in Massachusetts in the year 2000 (November).

Between mid-September and mid-November 1999, volunteers collected 118,500 signatures statewide. Berkshire County, birthplace of this new Abolition Movement, collected more signatures per population than any other county. This was an especially precarious referendum because it was the first time a state court had ruled that any extraneous marks on a petition could disqualify all the signatures on that sheet. On November 15th, 16th and 17th, the petitions were collected and driven by volunteers to the various city and town halls to be certified by city and town clerks. Boston was the one exception in that it was permitted to collect signatures for an additional week. During the last week in November, volunteers picked up the petitions from the city and town halls and drove them to the campaign office. The total amount certified by the city and town clerks was close to 90,000.

On December 1, 1999, the petitions were delivered to the Secretary of State's office in Boston and, after careful scrutiny, a total of 83,500 signatures were validated. Since only 57,000 were officially required, it appeared certain that the issue of banning dog racing would be on the ballot in November 2000.

In April 2000, the legislature ruled that more signatures would have to be collected. Although it had the authority to accept the already validated 83,500, it chose not to do so. We would have to collect an additional 9,700 signatures. And we did. Victories aren't simple matters, especially victories where lives compete with dollars. Victories over evil require a dream, total commitment to that dream, determination, and hard work. Even then there's no guarantee of success. We would learn this the hard way.

– June 2000

Ours was a winnable issue, yet we lost the election. We lost by a very small margin, less than 2%. This in itself demonstrates that the three large organizations were wrong. It was a small loss numerically speaking, but from the Greyhounds' perspective, it was a calamitous loss.

– December 2000

The next four pages show a variety of the materials used during the November 2000 Election Campaign.

Flier featuring Diana and Danny Boy. (Design by Ann Dennault; photo by G.M.)

Flier courtesy of G.M.

Poster courtesy of G.M.

This poster was widely used during the signature-collecting part of the election campaign in Massachusetts. The beautiful dog gazing at you is Shayna. (Designed by Chuck Cawley.)

Top: One of the five billboards posted throughout Massachusetts in Oct./Nov. 2000. (Shayna's face sketched by Joanne Hamilton.)

Billboard photo by Joanne Hamilton. Photo and poster courtesy of G.M.

Center: Another poster with the same information that was displayed in subway trains in eastern Massachusetts and in buses in western Massachusetts. (Designed by graphic artist Chuck Cawly.)

Bottom: A poster featuring local race car driver Bill Kirpens and Diana. (Designed by Sunshine Photos in Pittsfield, MA; photo by G.M.)

Poster courtesy of G.M.

STOP THE ABUSE!

STOP THE KILLING OF THE INNOCENT!

Each Year In The U.S., about 20,000 Greyhounds Are Put To Death/Murdered.

Please Vote YES On QUESTION 3, To Ban Dog Racing In Massachusetts.

Shayna

Flier by G.M.

It's time to stop all abuse and cruelty to

Greyhounds

Vote "YES"
Question 3
Nov. 7th

MASSACHUSETTS TRACK
GREYHOUND
DOES HE LOOK WELL CARED FOR?
Rescued : Spring 2000

Emaciated racing greyhound rescued
from a Local Massachusetts kennel

Postcard courtesy of John Cram.

PART FIVE

Thank You

Some Things to Think About

Whoever Saves a Single Life,
Is as if One Saves the Entire World.

– Talmud

Thank You

I gratefully thank the following individuals and organizations for their lifesaving commitment to these wonderful dogs and to all other animals, regardless of species:

• **Representative Shaun Kelly**, the perservering and committed young legislator who filed three bils to ban dog racing in Massachusetts. MaCADR and Greyhounds everywhere are forever grateful to him.

• **Libby Frattaroli**, **Steven Baer** and **Robin Norton**, Massachusetts Citizens Against Dog Racing (MaCADR) volunteers who joined me in 1996. Until then – for four long, lonely, difficult years – it was just Shayna and I. And I thank Libby for starting the first protest ever at a dog track in Massachusetts. Often during the first year it was only she who was present. I also thank Libby for her lifesaving dedication to a variety of other-specied animals; likewise Steve, especially for his commitment to incarcerated and tortured nonhuman primates.

• The **elegant former racers** who assembled across the street from the State House on the morning of March 16, 1999, just prior to the public hearing for *House Bill 1926*. They were wearing coats on which were printed: "Free at Last," "Now I Can Run on the Beach," "I'm One of the Lucky Ones" and "Race Cars, Not Me." The idea for the coats was Beverly Alba's, MaCADR volunteer, and they were created by Greyhound advocate Holly Pearson.

• **Chuck Cawley**, MaCADR volunteer, who created the magnificent posters that appeared in the subway cars in Boston. They explained why dog racing should be banned and asked the public to support *HB 3434,* then *HB 1926*. Shayna's lovely face and soulful eyes were featured on them. For the election campaign, Chuck created similar posters asking voters to "Vote Yes on Question 3."

• **Susan Netboy**, Greyhound Protection League founder. In addition to rescuing many thousands of former racers nationwide, Susan has done a magnificent job exposing dog racing for what it really is.

• **Joan Eidenger**, publisher and editor of the Greyhound Network News (GNN), a newsletter that details the plight of racers and former racers nation and worldwide. Joan and her husband rescued and adopted their first Greyhound in May 1975. He was a two-and-a-half-year-old fawn male who was scheduled to be put to death because (they were told) "he lost his initiative to race." In other words, because he stopped winning at the track. His name was Tracker.

• **Anne**, the animal control officer who rescued Shayna, and the anonymous caller who alerted her. Without them, Shayna never would have come into my life or, for that matter, into anyone else's life.

• **Louise Coleman**, Greyhound Friends in Hopkinton, MA. If not for Louise, Shayna would not have come into my life. And without Shayna, there would be no movement to end dog racing in Massachusetts. In addition, Louise has worked relentlessly on behalf of Greyhounds in Ireland and Spain.

• **Greyhound rescuers everywhere** including, but not limited to:

Lisa St. Pierre, Greyhound Friends West in Great Barrington, MA. Lisa and members of her group have come to the aid of former racers who needed immediate rescuing, and Lisa is responsible for bringing Diana into our lives after J.J. and Shayna's sudden departures.

Robin Norton, Greysland Greyhound Adoption in Hopkinton, MA. Robin rescues healthy Greyhounds as well as large numbers of seriously ill and seriously injured former racers who require intensive veterinary treatment and surgery. She is responsible for bringing Danny Boy into our lives after Murphy's very sudden departure.

Scotti Devens and Save The Greyhound Dogs! in Essex, VT. Scotti and her Greyhound, Gator, are responsible for the bill that ended dog racing in Vermont in 1995. She too has worked relentlessly on behalf of Greyhounds in Spain.

John Cram and Sandy Styman for rescuing so many former racers directly from the tracks.

Ann Shannon (Isle of Man, UK) for trying so hard to stop the sale of Irish Greyhounds to Spain. To date the sales continue.

Marion Fitzgibbons, president of the Irish SPCA, for working so hard to stop the sale of Irish Greyhounds to Spain where they die incredulous and brutal deaths. As noted, the sales continue to date.

Anne Finch, Greyhounds in Need (Surrey, England) for her incredible dedication and perseverance in rescuing former racers in England, Ireland and Spain.

The **Irish Council Against Blood Sports**, for its commitment to other-specied animals in Ireland.

Señor Fermín Peréz Martín, founder of Scooby, an organization and refuge dedicated to rescuing Greyhounds and galgos in Spain.

Election campaign volunteers for collecting more than enough signatures and guaranteeing us a place on the ballot in November, 2000. And for their dedication and committment during the campaign. They know who they are.

My friends at **Berkshire Advocates for Animals**, all of whom are very special and extraordinary persons and whose friendship I shall cherish forever, for their commitment to creatures of all species, large and small, and to the election campaign. They are: **Lynn Lavinio, Terry Carlo and Scott Plantier, Marnie Meyers, Dian Howe, Paulette Wein, Mary and Matt Kelly, Sheila and Jack Faxon, Debra and Michael Buratto, Liz Nichols, Cathy Groves** (who read Shayna's Story - Part One and made some valuable suggestions), and **Joanne Hamilton**. It was our mutual respect and love for horses and our determination to save them from slaughter, abuse and neglect that first brought Joanne and I together and started a friendship that will last forever.

The **Berkshire Humane Society** – president **Robert Fuster**, the **Board of Directors**, the **staff and volunteers** – for their commitment to and support of the election campaign. And a special thanks to **John Perrault**, shelter manager, for his commitment to and concern for these wonderful dogs – and for permitting me to use some very graphic photos he had taken. They were used state- and nationwide, and helped expose the awful truth about dog racing in New England.

Patrice and Kaare Bolgen (he was member of the Norwegian Underground during World War II) for all they have done for Greyhounds and other-specied animals throughout the years. It was the tragic plight of Greyhounds that initially brought us together and started a friendship that will last forever.

Erica Hartman, for all she has done for Greyhounds and other-specied animals for so many years. She is an animals' angel. Again, it was the Greyhounds who initially brought us together and started a friendship that will last forever.

Elaine Nash, who has rescued large numbers of other-specied animals, including horses. It was our mutual love and respect for these magnificent creatures that started a friendship that will last forever. Some, but not all, of our rescued horses were former racers.

Tamara More and friends of "Lev Le´Chai" in Tel Aviv for their passionate commitment to rescuing other-specied animals in Israel.

Mary and Kenneth Terry and staff of Turtle Rock Rescue, Fitzwilliam, NH, for their heroic rescues of domestic and wild horses and burros.

Kathleen Hofferty, wherever she may be, founder of the now-defunct Ipswich Equine Rescue in Ipswitch, MA, for her dedication and committment to Premarin foals and former race horses.

Susan Stanhope, a friend of all other-specied animals, especially horses, to whom I'm forever grateful. She knows why.

Paula Bonarrigo, for rescuing horses as well as other animals of different species; and **Ellen Gabes**, for the very same reason.

Lisa, Carol and Dick DeMayo, who patiently taught me the fundamentals of horse care. It was Lisa who brought Brody (former show horse), May (former Polo Pony) and Georgie Boy (former racer) into my life. All three were destined for slaughter. It was also through Lisa that I adopted a three-day-old calf, whom I named Minh.

Terry Cummings and **Dave Hoerauf**, founders of Poplar Spring Animal Sanctuary in Poolesville, MD, where Minh has resided since 1997. It is there that he discovered he's a cow, not a horse.

Laurie and Gene Bauston, founders of Farm Sanctuary, the first large-scale sanctuary for farm animals. It has shelters in NY and CA.

The Peace Abbey's **Meg and Lewis Randa** for their many rescues, among them Emily and Gloria, two cows who escaped from a local slaughterhouse.

Dylan Arnould, my thirteen-year-old grandson, for rescuing this manuscript from the mysterious bowels of my computer.

Larry Interlande of Crocker Communications, for graciously volunteering his technical expertise whenever I needed it.

Ann Dennault, for preparing the wonderful election campaign flier featuring Danny Boy and Diana.

The staff at **South Street Veterinary Services** in Pittsfield, MA, for permitting me to display a variety of literature on behalf of the three bills to end dog racing in Massachusetts, as well as the ballot initiative. And for their dedication and commitment to their clients.

Gwen and Tom Shaughnessy: Gwen for looking in on Murphy and Diana, and then Diana and Danny Boy, during the election campaign when I was absent for many hours of many days; Tom for reducing a poster of Shayna to postcard size, giving us another way of sending out our message.

The late and lovely **Denise (Nee Cee) Piroso**, activist and artist, who did so much for other-specied animals during her brief journey on Earth.

The late **Helen Jones**, founder of the International Society for Animal Rights (ISAR), who sent out the very first mass mailings on behalf of Rep. Kelly's first bill, *HB 899*.

I also thank:

- Everyone who has rescued or adopted a former racer, whether a Greyhound or a horse.
- Everyone who has rescued or adopted an animal in need, large or small, human or of another species.
- All the anonymous individuals and groups who quietly rescue other-specied animals and the no-kill shelters that help them.
- Researchers who practice ethical and valid science, and never have used animals of other species as research tools.
- Researchers who once did, but no longer do.
- Everyone who doesn't eat cadavers, meaning the flesh and body parts of murdered animals of other species.
- Everyone who still does, but has reduced the amount consumed, the goal being total abstinence.
- Everyone who doesn't wear the skins or fur of other-specied animals.
- Everyone who never hunted other-specied animals.
- Everyone who once did, but no longer does.
- Everyone who never attended a circus that uses other-specied animals.
- Everyone who once did, but no longer does.
- Circuses that don't use animals of other species. They are fascinating and exciting, the performers are exceptionally talented and skilled, and they are cruelty-free.
- Everyone who has never attended or participated in a rodeo.
- Everyone who once did, but no longer does.
- Everyone who has found the compassion and love that lies somewhere deep inside them and has never deliberately harmed a human or other-specied animal.
- Racers and former racers, Greyhounds and horses, nation- and worldwide, for loving us in spite of what some of us have done and continue to do to them.

- **J.J.**, our elder statesman, for being such an important part of our lives and Shayna's story, and for teaching us what dignity and nobility are all about.

- **Murphy**, my treasured companion for more than nine years, Shayna's best buddy, and an integral part of her story. Thank you Murphy, for bringing stability into my life and smiles to my face.

- **Diana**, adorable and precious, fun-loving and loving, for allowing the sun to shine again for Murphy and me after J.J. and Shayna left us so suddenly.

- **Danny Boy**, handsome and sleek, funny and so very precious, for pushing aside some of the clouds and allowing the sun to shine again for Diana and me after Murphy left us so very suddenly.

- And **Shayna**, for coming into my life, inspiring and motivating me, and changing my life forever. Without her there would be no movement to end dog racing in Massachusetts. She kept me focused even when things looked pretty glum, as they did more often than not. Sometimes I wonder if she's an angel whose mission on earth was to start this battle. Perhaps she left before it was finished because she was just meant to plant the seed. She did her job well. In the beginning it was just one person whom she inspired, then a few more, then hundreds more, and now many thousands.

To each and every one of you, I'm eternally grateful.

– Greta Marsh

(December 1999 –
December 2000)

SOME OF GRETA'S FRIENDS

Right: Brody, Greta's first rescued horse — a former show horse. Shown with Lisa De Mayo on the evening she brought him home to Greta's place. (August 27, 1992)

Below: Greta's friend Mara with Shayna out on the deck.

Photos by G.M.

Photos courtesy of Elaine Nash.

Above: Gabriel was rescued as a three-month-old foal. This photo was taken a few days after his rescue when he was infested with blood worms, intestinal parasites and lice. Note that Greta is wearing a fake fur coat with a large button that reads "Real People Wear Fake Fur" from the Fund for Animals. It's an eye-catcher and often a conversation starter. (Nov. 1996)

Left: Gabriel, beloved of Elaine Nash, waiting for her to come out and play. (May 2002)

Photos courtesy of Elaine Nash.

Above: Greta's granddaughter Holly with one of Elaine's equine friends. (Oct. 2002)

DEVOTED
BUDDIES

Left: Gabriel and Elaine Nash. (Autumn 2001)

MORE OF GRETA'S FRIENDS

Right: Snoopy — adorable, rescued at two years of age. His misshapen front leg doesn't stop him from running and having fun. (Sept. 2001)

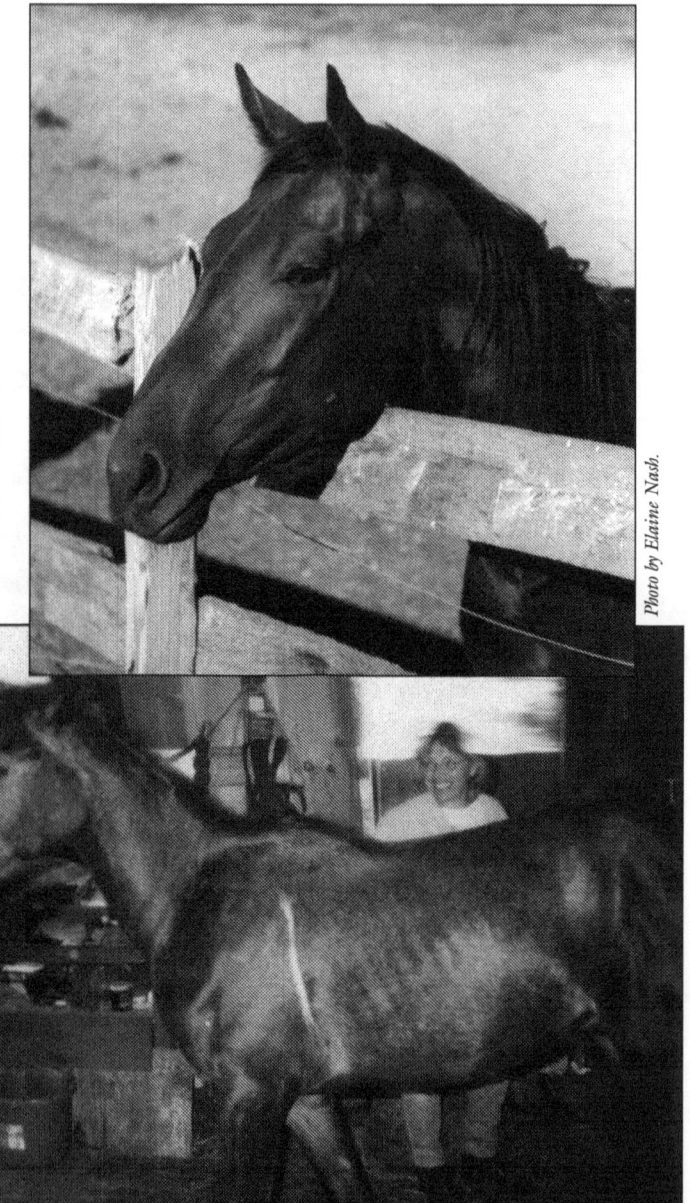

Photo by Elaine Nash.

Photo by G.M.

Above: Another rescued foal, nine months old, in his new home. Elaine Nash is in the background. (Spring 2001)

Photos by Matt & Mary Kelly.

Top: Matt Kelly and Henry, a rescued turkey.

Center: Lilly Hen and Daisy Calf, two of Mary and Matt's many rescues. (1999)

Bottom: Mary Kelly with Daisy, a rescued calf.

ANOTHER
LUCKY CALF

Photos courtesy of G.M.

Greta feeding Baby Albert —
a rescued calf. (1997)

Photos by G.M.

Above: Albert and Amber, Elaine Nash's granddaughter who was visiting from Ireland. (Sept. 1997)

Center: Caitlin, one of Greta's granddaughters, with Albert.

Bottom: Caitlin with her sister Meghan when Albert was six days old. (July 20, 1997)

MINH & FRIENDS

Right: Minh at 10 nomths old with Matt Kelley.

Bottom: Minh when he was two-and-a-half years old, just a few days before he went to live at Poplar Spring Animal Sanctuary n Poolesville, MD. (April 1997)

Both photos courtesy of G.M.
Bottom photo by Erika Hartman.

Ad courtesy of Pangea Products.

Minh is inteligent, adorable, lovable and quite a character.
As you can see, he is also a part-time model.

Seek Justice;
Relieve the Oppressed.

– Isaiah 1:17

Some Things to Think About

Dog racing is a lethal form of entertainment and a legal form of murder. As of August 2000, there were forty-nine tracks operating in fifteen states in the United States. As of 2002, there were forty-seven operating in fifteen states. As already noted, dog racing also is active in England, Wales, Scotland, Ireland, Spain, Italy, Macau, Philippines, Vietnam, Abu Dubai (one of seven states in the United Arab Emirates), Mexico, Australia, New Zealand, Guam (a territory of the U.S.) and even a city in war-devastated Bosnia. As more and more states in the U.S. pass laws banning dog racing (seven to date), this international industry attempts to introduce it into even more countries, especially third world countries (for example, South Africa). According to the GNN, Summer 2001, the latest countries to embrace it are Korea, China and Sweden. It's well-known that dogs are eaten in Korea and China, so we can anticipate the fate that awaits racers in those countries.

In the U.S. in 1998, about 35,000 Greyhound puppies were born, only about half of whom would ever reach a commercial track – the other half reportedly would have been put to death before reaching eighteen months of age. Over-breeding is rampant and practiced in the hopes of obtaining some champions, and to make certain there always are a sufficient number of youngsters to replace injured, older and no-longer-profitable racers. Some are put to death by lethal injection. But, because it can cost $25 or more per dog, many are killed by cheap, brutal and painful methods.

In Maine (1993) and Virginia (1995), bills were passed making dog racing illegal. It should be noted that there were no dog tracks in these states and dog racing never had been active in either one of them. In 1995, dog racing was made illegal in Vermont, where it no longer was active – its only dog track in Pownal had closed in December 1992, after a cruelty investigation. In 1996, dog racing was banned in Idaho, where it no longer was active – its only track had closed in December 1995, after an exposé of electrocutions and other forms of killing triggered a criminal investigation. In 1997, dog racing was banned in the state of Washington, where there were no dog tracks and dog racing never was active. That same year it was made illegal in Nevada, where it once was active for just a year – its only track opened in January 1981 and closed in December of that same year.

Finally, in 1998, dog racing was made illegal in North Carolina. Between 1945 and 1953, it was active in two North Carolina counties. In 1954, however, the state Supreme Court ruled that the two county laws establishing it violated the state constitution and therefore were void. When it appeared that dog racing might be rekindled in North Carolina, concerned persons got busy and the state legislature passed a law prohibiting both live and simulcast dog racing.

It was in Massachusetts, however, that the first bills were filed to ban dog racing in a state where it still was legal and active. Consequently, although the three bills (filed in 1994, 1996 and 1998) were popular with large numbers of Massachusetts citizens, they weren't popular with the committee that oversees state gambling and racing issues. Loss of revenue and jobs were cited as the reasons.

The first two bills were sent to study committees, where they quietly died without ever having been debated or voted on by the House or Senate. Because we believed the same fate awaited the third bill (filed in December 1998), MaCADR and other Greyhound advocates decided the ballot was the only other way to go. As already noted, we lost the election.

It is to be hoped that someday animals of other species will be granted the rights due all living beings. This is not wishful thinking because it wasn't so very long ago that large numbers of white persons, threatened by the notion that black persons should have the same rights they had, insisted that black persons were not really persons. They were sub-humans, less-than-persons, they said.

Why? Because they believed slaves were essential to the economy of the American South, that without them the Southern economy would collapse. Not only did they insist that black persons were sub-humans, they said they could not feel pain, could not suffer, were incapable of feeling any emotions and lacked souls. These are the same arguments people use to justify the pain, torture and deliberate killing of animals of other species. Proponents of these arguments likewise insist that this torture and killing of other-specied animals are vital to the economy of the human-centered community.

But animals of other species experience joy, sadness, pain and fear just as we do. And they suffer just as we do. If we possess souls, then so do they. And until we start treating them as beings who are deserving of respect, consideration and compassion, the world we live in will continue to be turbulent, brutal, violent and unsafe for all of its inhabitants.

"Woe to those who build their house by unjust means
and their upper rooms by injustice."

– Gates of Prayer
The New Union Prayerbook
Central Conference of American Rabbis
(New York, 1975)

About the Author

Since her teenage years, Greta Marsh has been active in the human civil rights movement. Her Master's Thesis was a comprehensive study of racial violence and discrimination in the United States and the founding of the NAACP (National Association for the Advancement of Colored People) in 1909 by African and European Americans. In August 1963, she participated in Martin Luther King Jr.'s March on Washington for Jobs and Freedom.

For many years, Greta was a probation officer and worked with troubled, abused and neglected children, battered women, and an occasional battered man. Then, in the early 1980s, she crossed the barrier that separates the species and became an advocate not just for human animals, but for other-specied animals as well.

Upon retiring from the Nassau County, NY, Probation Department in late 1991, Greta moved to Lanesboro, MA, and started rescuing horses (and some calves and cats, too). It was lovely Shayna who inspired and motivated her to take an active stand against dog racing, which changed Greta's life forever.

Greta is the mother of five, the grandmother of seven. She and Diana and Danny Boy now reside in Easthampton, MA.

www.ingramcontent.com/pod-product-compliance
Lightning Source LLC
Chambersburg PA
CBHW032142020726
47496CB00003B/679